# CHECKMATE

## A Play on Murder

## by Leslie Sands

# SAMUEL FRENCH, INC.

45 WEST 25TH STREET      NEW YORK 10010
7623 SUNSET BOULEVARD      HOLLYWOOD 90046
*LONDON*      *TORONTO*

## IMPORTANT BILLING AND CREDIT REQUIREMENTS

# CHARACTERS

PETER CONWAY

STELLA CONWAY

SGT DRUMMOND

LORI NILSSON

RICHARD SHAW

BBC DRESSER (non-speaking)

TV VOICE (female, unseen)

# SCENE

An attractive mews-cottage, situated not far from
the Thames Embankment in London.

# SYNOPSIS OF SCENES

## ACT I

Scene 1: Friday afternoon
Scene 2: One hour later

## ACT II

Scene 1: After midnight
Scene 2: The next morning

# AUTHOR'S NOTES

a) During the "thought-sequences" in this play the stage lighting should be tinged with blue, to keep the action the merest touch away from reality.

b) The use of a strong musical theme (as indicated) will greatly assist in the cohesion of the plot's development.

c) This haunting music should also be played throughout the short scene-drop that occurs in each Act.

L.S.

# CHECKMATE

## ACT I

### Scene 1

*SETTING: The story is told at Peter Conway's home in one of the more exclusive residential areas of the capital. At first sight the living room may seem luxurious to the point of extravagance, but closer examination would reveal that nowadays some of its lush trappings are growing rather seedy.*

*The front door U.C. opens onstage from an attractive porch outside, with a glimpse of flowers and well-chosen shrubs. U.R. is a bar structure, complete with hidden handbasin for rinsing glasses and etcetera. Thickly carpeted steps U.L. lead to a square landing that gives access to the upper rooms, which are out of view on a split-level, off-L. The kitchen is off-R. and is reached by a swing-door that has been padded to keep out extraneous noise. In the centre of the LEFT WALL tall, richly curtained windows open on to a patio that scans a broad sweep of London's river.*

*There are two concealed doors, one D.L. and the other D.R; however, we shall not be aware of the existence of these until they are brought to our notice during the course of the action.*

*Décor and furnishings are a discreet mix of Sanderson's, Heal's and the better shops in Chelsea; and there is strong evidence of a consuming interest in the Theatre in well-chosen posters and playbills, theatrical memorabilia, bric-â-brac and the like.*

*The main feature of the RIGHT WALL is a photo blow-up of Peter Conway in his favourite role of "Inspector Savage" (a once-popular TV hero) mounted on the wall above an expensive hi-fi installation.*

*AT RISE: Friday. The THEME-MUSIC from the "Savage" television series is playing softly. The room is peaceful and quiet in half-light. The main curtains are drawn.*

*PETER CONWAY, a well-known actor on stage and screen, comes down the stairs. HE is a well set-up man in his early forties, good-looking and gifted with great personal charm and a forceful personality.*

*HE pauses to look back in the direction of the bedroom, before crossing and sitting at his desk to use the telephone.*

*HE dials 999.*

*FADE THEME MUSIC*

PETER. Give me the police. 577-2609. Thank you. *(HE passes a hand across his forehead as HE waits for a moment.)* Hello—my name is Peter Conway. I'm calling from 2a, Dover Mews. I'm—afraid there's been a serious accident here. My wife. I just came in and found her ... *(Breaks off; then:)* I'm afraid so, yes. Thank you. No, I won't touch anything. *(HE hangs up. After checking the time by his watch, HE gets up and goes to a cloaks cupboard near the front door; from here HE takes out a smart sheepskin coat—his own—and goes carefully through the pockets. They are empty except for a pair of thin leather driving-gloves. HE puts these back where they came from, and sets the car-coat over one end of the settee. HE returns to the phone, this time using it from a standing position and punching up numbers from memory.*) Richard, please. It's Peter Conway—Christ Almighty, don't you know my voice by now? No, I can't hold. I don't give a damn *who* he's with: I want Richard Shaw and I want him *now. (HE waits, impatiently.)* What do you mean, "not at his desk"? He's always there bang on nine o'clock. *(Pause).* No, thanks! *(HE slams the phone down.)*

*(HE gets up and crosses to the bar, where HE pours himself a large brandy. HE is just about to take a sip when a KNOCK comes at the door.*
*PETER leaves his glass and goes to answer it.*
*DRUMMOND is on the doorstep—a pleasant, unassuming Londoner of indeterminate age, with a wrinkled face, a dry voice, and a somewhat salty sense of humour.)*

DRUMMOND. Drummond, sir. *(Shows warrant-card.)* CID.
    PETER. That was quick.
    DRUMMOND. We're only just round the corner—
    PETER. Come in, sergeant.

*(The POLICEMAN throws him a glance—he has not mentioned his rank—before coming down into the room. HE drags loose the Chelsea F.C. scarf he habitually wears.)*

DRUMMOND. Even coppers can move fast, you know—given time. Though as I understand it, the accident was fatal?

PETER. Yes. Upstairs.

DRUMMOND. You're quite sure she's dead, sir?

PETER. I tested.

DRUMMOND. (*No time-waster.*) Bedroom?

PETER. That's right.

(*HE tries to follow, as DRUMMOND makes for the stairs.*)

PETER. I found her myself, just five minutes ago.

DRUMMOND. (*Turning.*) You didn't touch anything, did you?

PETER. They told me not to.

DRUMMOND. Leave this to me then, please. I know my way around. (*HE goes off upstairs.*)

(*PETER hovers for a moment, as if uncertain of what to do next; then HE goes to the bar, to take a sip of the brandy HE poured earlier on.*

*Carrying his glass to the desk, HE sits and picks up the phone again, stabbing at buttons quickly. This time HE gets through immediately.*)

PETER. Richard? It's Peter. Look, that appointment this morning—it'll have to be cancelled. I don't know, tell 'em I'm not available. Yes Richard, I know it's important and—I know, I know—I'm not turning my nose up at anything, I—will you for God's sake shut up and listen? (*HE pauses briefly before carrying on, now more in control.)* Stella's dead. It looks like an overdose. No, I can't believe it either. *(Quietly.)* Yes, they're here now. Don't come; it wouldn't help. I'll call you. *(HE hangs up. His glance travels to a large, silver-framed photograph of his wife that always stands on the desk, matched by his own framed picture. HE picks up Stella's, and gazes at it sadly.)*

*(DRUMMOND reappears on the landing.)*

    PETER. *(Whispers.)* Why, Stella ... why?
    DRUMMOND. Excuse me, sir—

*(PETER looks up from his wife's portrait, his mind still on her.)*

    DRUMMOND. *(With quiet respect.)* I used the phone in the bedroom—hope you don't mind?
    PETER. That's what it's there for.
    DRUMMOND. The lads'll be here soon: they'll take care of everything.
    PETER. Yes. No hurry, is there? Not now.
    DRUMMOND. I suppose not.

*(PETER sets the picture back in position.)*

    DRUMMOND. I'd try to relax, if I were you. Easier said than done, I know.
    PETER. Too true.
    DRUMMOND. *(Takes out cheap cigarettes, toying with the packet awkwardly.)* May I—express my sympathies, sir? I liked Mrs. Conway very much.

PETER. Thank you. She was the right sort. (*HE crosses to the windows to stare out, speaking over his shoulder and trying his hardest to appear normal.*) I seem to know your face. Met before, have we?

DRUMMOND. You knew I was a sergeant as well; I never said.

PETER. What's your name again?

DRUMMOND. Drummond, sir. Bill Drummond.

PETER. Rings a bell.

DRUMMOND. It should: I was here a couple of years ago when you had this place turned over.

PETER. (*Turns.*) The burglary—of course.

DRUMMOND. You were busy at the studios and your wife was out, when three lads from Stepney broke in here and helped themselves. They even had a drink or two while they were at it. That's what nailed 'em.

PETER. Fingerprints, yes. (*Remembering.*) On two glasses.

DRUMMOND. I collared 'em and put 'em away for you. Happy ending. Only wish I could supply the same on this occasion. Can I smoke?

PETER. Help yourself. There's some on the desk.

DRUMMOND. I'll stick to my own, thanks. If I start switching brands, I cough me heart out. (*Opens packet.*) Not that these are up to much—three parts coal tar to one of camel dung. (*Offers them.*) Try one?

PETER. No, thanks.

DRUMMOND. Don't blame you. Still, it helps the concentration, so they tell me.

PETER. That means it's question-time.

DRUMMOND. 'Fraid so. Sudden Death Report.

PETER. Form 44.

DRUMMOND. I was forgetting. You know the drill, don't you? (*HE lights up and it makes him cough, immediately.*) Like to sit down, sir?

PETER. I talk better standing up.

DRUMMOND. I don't. (*Takes a seat.*) Funny—I've been a copper ever since I left school, but somehow it's one thing you never quite get used to, sudden death. Shakes you. Does me, anyway.

PETER. Understandable.

DRUMMOND. Oh, I dunno! Look at you, you're as cool as a cucumber.

PETER. (*Not immediately.*) I'm not feeling it, sergeant.

DRUMMOND. How d'you manage it?

PETER. I happen to be an actor: it's part of my job to keep personal feelings well under control.

DRUMMOND. But you're not acting now, are you?

PETER. (*Oddly.*) How would you know?

DRUMMOND. (*Coughs again.*) Quite. We could nip round to the station if you'd rather—

PETER. No. I'll go through this in my own home. Stella would have preferred it.

DRUMMOND. Up to you. (*Takes out notebook.*) Right—Question One. Did you have any idea at all that she was contemplating suicide?

PETER. None whatever. When I left here yesterday I'd have said nothing was further from her mind.

DRUMMOND. Question Two—

PETER. (*Bluntly.*) Why didn't they send a squad car? That's more usual, isn't it?

DRUMMOND. Busy morning, Fridays—I've been on the go all night. I was in the station waiting for my relief when the shout came through. Knowing you, I thought I'd give it the personal touch.

PETER. I appreciate that.

DRUMMOND. (*Grins.*) Besides—a feather in anybody's cap, isn't it, looking after Peter Conway?

PETER. You reckon?

DRUMMOND. Goes without saying. Now then, Question Two. How was the incident discovered?

PETER. I got into Victoria half an hour ago, and picked up a cab at the station—

DRUMMOND. Been away, have you?

PETER. Only for the night. I must have walked in here a few minutes after nine o'clock.

DRUMMOND. It was eight minutes past exactly when you phoned in.

PETER. In the Occurrence Book, is it?

DRUMMOND. Too right.

PETER. However, I didn't find Stella straightaway. *(HE begins to track his former movements about the room, as if keen for these to be accurately noted.)* I let myself in at the front door and put my coat down here. I called her name out but there was no reply. I was surprised to find the curtains still drawn—*(HE goes back to the windows.)*

DRUMMOND. Early riser, was she?

PETER. My wife doesn't—*(Corrects himself.)*—she *didn't* sleep well. *(HE makes as if to pull them back.)*

DRUMMOND. Leave 'em as they are, sir—till my lads have been.

PETER. But nothing at all happened down here—

DRUMMOND. Can't be sure, can we? Not till they've had a look-round.

PETER. Sorry, I wasn't thinking. *(HE comes away.)*

DRUMMOND. Still, I don't see why we shouldn't have a bit of light on the subject, as long as we're careful. (*HE rises and crosses to the door, using the end of his scarf to cover his hand as HE operates the switch. Then HE comes back to his chair.*)

PETER. I switched the radio on, to keep track of the time—

DRUMMOND. Any particular reason?

PETER. Yes; I had an important appointment fixed for half-past ten this morning: that's why I came back.

DRUMMOND. I'd cancel that, if I were you.

PETER. I already have. I was on the phone to my agent while you were upstairs.

DRUMMOND. Just as well.

PETER. Then I called out again, louder this time. I was going to make a cup of tea but when she still didn't answer, I thought better of it and went up to wake her. Those things she used to take were pretty lethal. (*HE breaks off suddenly.*)

DRUMMOND. (*Gently.*) And you found your wife dead when you entered the bedroom?

PETER. (*With a nod.*) Slumped across the divan, just as she is now. It wasn't natural. I remember wondering why she was still in a dressing-gown. I went over to her and said "Stella." Then I touched her. Cold as ice. It was after that I noticed the tablets—well, the empty bottle—by the bed. Excuse me. (*HE sinks into an armchair, putting his head in his hands.*)

DRUMMOND. Can I get you a drink, sir?

PETER. I've just had a brandy. (*Looks up.*) No, let's get this over with as quick as we can. I came back down here, turned off the radio and rang for help. I think that's all I can tell you.

DRUMMOND. It never occurred to you to ring a doctor?

PETER. No. (*Murmuring.*) I should have thought of that. (*Louder.*) But I was in such a state, you see. Anyway, you've been in there, sergeant: she was beyond medical aid.

DRUMMOND. (*Becomes more brisk and official-sounding, as HE takes notes.*) Could I have the full name, please?

PETER. Stella Conway. No other first names.

DRUMMOND. Conway's for real, is it—not just a stage-name?

PETER. I was born with it.

DRUMMOND. (*Nods.*) How old was she, sir?

PETER. Thirty-seven.

DRUMMOND. She wasn't in your line of business herself by any chance?

PETER. An actress? No. When we met, Stella was a personnel manager with the Beeb.

DRUMMOND. With the—?

PETER. The BBC.

DRUMMOND. Thank you.

PETER. She soon packed that in when I began to earn decent money, and looking after Peter Conway became a full-time job.

DRUMMOND. She didn't mind that? I mean, she wasn't jealous in any way of your success?

PETER. Good Lord, no. We were happily married, sergeant. Besides, where I come from the man of the house is supposed to be the breadwinner.

DRUMMOND. But you know what women are these days—Lib and Let Lib.

PETER. (*Absently.*) What?

DRUMMOND. Joke, sir. Meant to be. *(Philosophically.)* I'll never learn.

PETER. (*Ignoring this.*) Stella was very old- fashioned in her ways. She came from the countryside as a matter of fact—a clergyman's daughter.

DRUMMOND. Strict upbringing, then. That doesn't usually tie in with a thing like this. Can she have been worried about her health, d'you suppose? (*As PETER shakes his head.*) Women don't always say, do they?

PETER. I think I'd have known, after ten years of being married to her.

DRUMMOND. You did mention she was on sleeping-pills—

PETER. Repposal.

DRUMMOND. Strong as you'll get ... sixty percent phenobarbitone. What brought that on?

PETER. Overstrain. She hated this house and she hated London. She was always on at me to move; and I was always telling her actors have to live where the work is.

DRUMMOND. Makes sense. (*Blows smoke out.*) Stays with you all your life though, doesn't it? Upbringing, I mean. I was dragged up in the Mile End Road; if I take a holiday in the countryside, I can't sleep for the birds!

PETER. My wife was under the doctor for hypertension; nothing else.

DRUMMOND. We'll need his name for details.

PETER. I have a card somewhere. (*HE goes to the desk to search.*)

DRUMMOND. (*Casually*.) Was Mrs. Conway well-insured, sir? Er—Form 44's pretty comprehensive.

(*Brief pause.*)

PETER. We were cross-insured for fifty thousand pounds.

DRUMMOND. Life, or accident?

PETER. Both.

DRUMMOND. You'll benefit by the death then, in a manner of speaking?

PETER. I've no idea. I expect self-destruction makes a hell of a difference.

DRUMMOND. They can load the premiums—

PETER. I couldn't care less. Here's the medical card. (*HE hands the doctor's details over for Drummond to read.*)

DRUMMOND. Local man; that helps.

PETER. Next question?

DRUMMOND. Mental state, sir. Any signs of acute depression or insecurity?

PETER. Take a look around. What would you say?

DRUMMOND. I'd say the family were doing pretty well.

PETER. There is no family, sergeant. Just Stella and me. That was one of our biggest disappointments.

DRUMMOND. Mews cottage—smashing conversion—up-market area. What more could any woman want?

PETER. Stella wasn't just "any woman."

DRUMMOND. (*Goes on.*) Different in my case. I'm the genuine article—a real, live, honest-to-God copper. All I can afford is a police-house on the wrong side of the river, curtains run up on the wife's sewing-machine and a three-piece suite in dralon on the never-never. We've never known what it is to have fitted carpets! And three kids at the council school, all going the same way. Like they say at the Old Bailey, there ain't no justice!

PETER. (*Humouring him.*) You may be right.

DRUMMOND. Just look at all this, though! (*Glancing about him.*) Where've you hidden that great big telly you used to have?

PETER. It's built-in now, at the bar.

DRUMMOND. Ask a silly question! Bang and Olufsen, as I remember, and very pricey—like the hi-fi. Got it made, haven't you, sir? Great big BMW out in the garage, I shouldn't wonder?

PETER. (*Smiles.*) It's a Porsche.

DRUMMOND. I might have known. Out in that last night, were you?

PETER. No. I travelled by train.

(*DRUMMOND is still gazing about in admiration, as PETER discreetly changes the subject.*)

PETER. None of this came overnight, you know.

DRUMMOND. I'm not saying it did! Tough life show business, by all accounts.

PETER. They don't come any tougher. (*With an edge.*) Eighty-five per cent unemployment problem, permanently. And no pension at the end of it. Unlike the police.

DRUMMOND. But you beat the odds, didn't you, Mr. Conway? Right to the very top. My wife's a tremendous fan of yours—all the kids, as well. I was never allowed out on a Friday night when you were on the telly! When's it coming back, that police series of yours?

PETER. Inspector Savage? (*Carefully.*) Nothing's been decided.

DRUMMOND. Playing hard to get, are we? (*Taps nose.*) Know which side the bread's buttered, eh? Keep 'em waiting till you're good and ready—and meanwhile, take a nice long vacation. Is that it?

PETER. We call it "resting" in the profession.

DRUMMOND. So I've heard.

PETER. That's going to be my epitaph: "Peter Conway, actor. Resting—as usual."

DRUMMOND. (*Tickled.*) Have to laugh, don't you?

PETER. Whenever you can, sergeant, believe me. (*It is his turn to let his gaze roam round the room.*) You're right about it sticking with you, though—background, I mean. My father was an artisan in the Black Country. He made roof-tiles, all his working life. He died at fifty-five of asbestosis. That wasn't going to happen to me.

DRUMMOND. Fond of the old man, were you?

PETER. I worshipped him.

DRUMMOND. Strange I don't see any family photographs about ...

PETER. I kept one thing of his, just to remind me. (*HE goes to some shelves on the wall at the rear, and takes down a slim leather case that is worn and stained. HE displays its contents.*)

DRUMMOND. What do you know? One of your old cut-throat razors.

PETER. Twenty-first birthday present; he used it all his life.

DRUMMOND. Pearl-handled, an' all!

PETER. It's got his initials, see? Just there. "G.C."— George Conway.

DRUMMOND. You couldn't put a price on that nowadays—

PETER. I'd never part with it. (*HE puts the souvenir back where it belongs.*)

DRUMMOND. He must have been real proud of you—seeing you on the telly, and all that—big star part—

PETER. He died; just before the breaks came.

DRUMMOND. Hard lines. (*Leans back.*) Do you know, I can remember back to when Inspector Savage first started!

PETER. So can I. Only too well. We were renting a couple of sleazy rooms in bedsit land. You're a Londoner—are you familiar with West Hampstead? It's a sort of S-bend with fish-and-chip shops. Then one glorious night in June, they showed the pilot. That was on a Friday night, too. (*HE is walking slowly down on to the forestage, as he goes back in time.*) The next morning, bells were ringing all over London. My agent, Richard Shaw, went raving mad. I had to hang up on him, just to stop him talking!

*(Behind him, DRUMMOND has become lost in shadow.)*

PETER. Afterwards, I stood there in the sitting-room, trying to make myself believe that what had happened had really *happened*. (*By now HE is D.L.C.*) Stella came out of the kitchen. In those days she spent most of her time in there, making something out of nothing ...

*(The concealed door D.L. opens, to reveal a dingy kitchen backing.*
*His WIFE enters, wearing overall and headscarf. SHE is young, sparkling, and very much in love.)*

STELLA. Lunch is on, darling—mystery omelette. Yours is ready.

PETER. Just coming.

STELLA. Who rang?

*(HE looks at her. All at once, HE is a younger PETER— completely dazed by his sudden good fortune.)*

PETER. I'm not sure, but I think it was Father Christmas. He was raving on about a twelve-month contract, and options for another three years. About Press interviews and publicity stills. And about how, after the first series—and there should be more to come—we can go on the holiday of a lifetime. Do we like round-the-world cruises? And how do we fancy two new cars? One for weekdays, and keep the best for Sundays, and lunch at Number Ten!

STELLA. Have you gone round the bend?

PETER. Probably.

STELLA. Who *rang*?

PETER. Richard.

STELLA. *(Brightens.)* That must mean they liked the show—

PETER. Liked it? They're over the moon! Even the Big White Chief himself—he's crazy about it!

STELLA. *Zimmermann*? You impressed Zimmermann—the head of Famous Artists?

PETER. I've got him just where I want him. The BBC's been bending his ear all morning—

STELLA. They want the whole series?

PETER. They can't wait! Ten beautiful episodes and that's only for starters. Five thousand quid an episode, with masses of options to come and the pay going up by leaps and bounds—

STELLA. (*SHE flings herself into his arms.*) God bless Richard the Lionheart—

PETER. God bless Inspector Savage! (*HE kisses her in celebration.*) Now I can keep you in the manner to which you've never been accustomed—

STELLA. Who's complaining?

PETER. First off, we *move*. We're getting out of this place with the speed of light—

STELLA. If we do that, we can tell the landlord what we really think of him!

PETER. No more mice—no more superannuated geysers—no more communal loos on the landing—

STELLA. No more *grime*. Oh, golly!

PETER. What?

STELLA. Your omelette!

*(SHE scrambles off, and HE closes the door behind her. Then HE strolls back upstage, to Drummond.)*

DRUMMOND. End of the rainbow, eh? The pot of gold.

PETER. That's what it seemed like. After years and years of struggling and *surviving*. (*Ironically.*) That's what an actor's life's all about: ten percent talent, and ninety percent sheer bloody stamina.

DRUMMOND. But you made it.

PETER. The leading part in a great big TV series— wham, bam, thank you mam! People smiling at you for a change, knowing who you are. Tradesmen and bank-managers actually *welcoming* you, would you believe? Well, I'd worked for it, I'd earned it—and I damn well set out to enjoy it. D'you blame me?

DRUMMOND. When people see a real copper coming down the road they cross over, sharpish! Blame you, sir? I envy you.

PETER. Don't be too quick off the mark. (*Sits again.*) Because fame—and it was fame, of a sort—has its fair share of drawbacks. First, you don't belong to yourself any more: you're public property. The GBP gobble you up in no time.

DRUMMOND. Come again, sir?

PETER. The Great British Public, damn their eyes. I had three-and-a-half years of it—thirty-six episodes. Thirty bloody six! And every one a winner, so they told me.

DRUMMOND. They were right —you're a big name!

PETER. (*Levelly.*) No, sergeant. I used to be. They call it the bitch goddess, success. Well something bitched us up good and proper. Don't ask me what it was, ask the man in the street—or better still, the BBC's Research Department. All I know is, Inspector Savage suffered a sudden death of his own, two years ago. And there were no memorial services—no repeats. Since then—you might as well know—it's been hairy for Stella and me; bloody hairy.

DRUMMOND. They don't print everything in the papers, do they?

PETER. Not unless it has news value. I lost mine when Inspector Savage went right down the drain.

(*A beat.*)

DRUMMOND. Form 44 goes on to talk about "social and financial worries."

PETER. (*Throws him a hard look, and then rises to move about the room.*) They dropped the whole series without warning. I'd been living well, I admit that—you have to on that level, it's expected. Suddenly, and this is in confidence, I was out in the cold again. That's when you know who your friends are, when nobody wants to speak to you; apart from the building society and the income tax inspector.

DRUMMOND. Being out of work's no crime—

PETER. It is if you're an actor. You can't take any part that comes along, you see, not when you've been top of the ratings. Lower your standards and you're on the skids; and that only leads one way—downhill.

DRUMMOND. How did all this affect Mrs. Conway—if you don't mind me asking?

PETER. She'd got used to a certain life-style and found it difficult to accept change. I'm afraid she began to look for consolation.

DRUMMOND. Other men?

PETER. No, never. Something much more simple and convenient.

DRUMMOND. There's one final question on the 44. "Was the deceased of a respectable and temperate character?"

*(This gets no response.)*

DRUMMOND. There's a whisky decanter by her bedside, sir. It's empty.

PETER. It doesn't seem fair, crying Stella down when she's no longer here to—

DRUMMOND. (*Reminds him.*) We could easily have done this at the station—

PETER. I know, my choice. (*It all comes tumbling out.*) It wasn't her fault, you see: she'd been living under great stress while the series was on. One day she said to me "When do I ever *see* you?" It wasn't till then that I realised what was going on. Then when the bad times began to roll, things got worse and worse; till in the end, we were tearing each other apart.

DRUMMOND. It fits the pattern.

PETER. Recently I've had to cut back to the bone—had to. It led to a sort of flashpoint yesterday, and I ... I ... (*Tails off.*) Stella had been out in town all day and I'd been cooped up here, getting lower and lower. I was sitting in the armchair over here when she got back. And I can tell you she was in quite a temper ...

*(STELLA comes in by the front door, flinging it shut behind her. SHE is older now, metallically harder, and beautifully groomed.*
*DRUMMOND watches the proceedings from near the windows, remaining throughout in total silence and stillness.)*

PETER. Hello, love; you're back early.

*(Without answering, STELLA shrugs out of her coat and helps herself to a cigarette.)*

STELLA. Was it absolutely necessary? And if so— couldn't you at least have warned me?

PETER. (*Rises.*) What are you talking about?

STELLA. *You.* Closing my accounts all over London—cancelling credit-cards—making me a laughing-stock wherever I go—

PETER. I *did* warn you. I told you weeks and weeks ago—

STELLA. I get sick of all that whingeing! Maybe I stopped listening.

PETER. I was only being sensible; one of us has to be.

STELLA. Been to Barclay's again, have we? I know that look. "I talked to the bank-manager but he's playing hard to get."

PETER. Dead right. Only this time, there's no credit left; not a sou.

STELLA. Thanks to me?

PETER. Mainly, yes. I started cutting back as soon as I had to—

STELLA. Cue violins!

PETER. You've gone on ordering stuff hand over fist—

STELLA. Who's always telling me to keep up appearances? Who's dinned it into me, "never be poor and *look* poor"? I refuse to go round London looking as tatty as I feel!

PETER. There's a limit, Stell; we crashed through it a long time ago.

STELLA. Big deal—as they say in all your television scripts. (*SHE crosses to the bar to pour herself a large drink of white wine.*)

PETER. I've had a final demand from the wine merchants, as well.

STELLA. So how are we supposed to live from now on—correction, to exist?

PETER. Anything we need—repeat, *need*—we pay for, cash on the nail. Anything else, we do without.

STELLA. Back to those happy days—

PETER. Try it any other way and I'm headed for bankruptcy.

STELLA. (*Throws herself into a chair, and glares defiance at him.*) So what's the plot?

PETER. The way things are the bank can't help, and I don't blame 'em. On the other hand, they want to be sympathetic.

STELLA. Of course! All fans of yours, weren't they, once upon a time?

PETER. They're willing to advance us enough to live on against this house, until it can be sold.

STELLA. Say that again.

PETER. You heard.

STELLA. (*As her smile fades.*) Sell the house?

*(Her HUSBAND sits near her.)*

PETER. We don't need a place this size. You know what the upkeep's like.

STELLA. Not since you've been handling the housekeeping—

PETER. Even with property values as they are, I'm hoping we can make enough to pay our debts and find somewhere smaller to live, cheaper to run—

STELLA. Back to bedsit land, is it?

PETER. (*Looks at her.*) We had good times in the old days, as well as bad—

STELLA. We *made* the good times out of nothing, because we were sweating it out to a purpose.

PETER. Look, we hit a bad patch! All actors have 'em.

STELLA. They don't all end up in Carey Street. Big man—big finish.

PETER. (*Rises, moving away from her.*) I'm nothing big at all, and never was. I don't even call myself an actor any more. Just a jumped-up television name. Ten a penny.

STELLA. You're not even that now, my darling; otherwise they'd still be after you.

*(PETER gives up, with an audible sigh. His back is to her, as SHE rises to go and refill her glass.)*

PETER. Leave it alone Stell, please.

STELLA. Why? It's the only thing that makes any sense out of my rotten life. (*Picks up coat.*) If you think I'm going back to two stinking rooms in West Hampstead, you can think again.

PETER. What's your solution?

STELLA. Go my own way. A pleasant change that after all these years of going yours! (*SHE takes her drink off with her to the bedroom.*)

*(PETER looks beaten and sad, as DRUMMOND moves in to join him.)*

PETER. If only I'd known what she meant—really meant—I'd never have left here yesterday.

DRUMMOND. It's understandable.

PETER. I tried to reason with her but it was hopeless. She hit the bottle good and hard, and only became more and more abusive. In the end—I had to go.

DRUMMOND. Where to, sir?

PETER. Is that important?

DRUMMOND. Possibly … in view of this.

*(HE takes from his inside pocket a postcard-sized photograph of a lovely young girl, and holds it out.)*

DRUMMOND. Luscious, isn't she?

PETER. Where the devil did you get that?

DRUMMOND. From your wife's dressing-table. *(Sets it down.)* Along with this. *(HE produces a plain gold ring.)*

DRUMMOND. Wedding ring. Mrs. Conway's I shouldn't wonder, in view of the fact that she's no longer wearing one.

PETER. Oh, my God.

DRUMMOND. You didn't notice either of these while you were up there?

PETER. I wasn't searching the room, sergeant; I never went near the dressing-table. *(HE sinks into a seat again.)*

DRUMMOND. Take it easy, sir: you've had a bit of a jolt, one way and another.

PETER. I never dreamt she knew. Knew that—*(His head goes into his hands again.)*

DRUMMOND. Maybe you should have told me all about the girl.

PETER. *(Looks up at him.)* I was trying to keep that part of it out of the papers. *(Confesses.)* There's been another girl for a long time now ... not always with the same name.

DRUMMOND. This one signs herself with the initial "L." Sends all her love. That indicates you knew each other fairly well?

PETER. Intimately. (*HE rises, as if to face up to this new situation.*) Lori was in the last episode of Savage we ever made. (*HE starts to stroll D.C.*) I met her at the studios. They call it the dream factory.

*(We hear SOUND EFFECTS of a television studio in action, during a short break in recording.*
*PETER is now isolated in a pool of LIGHT.*
*A TELEVISION VOICE booms out at us, over amplifiers. It is female, stentorian and impersonal.)*

TV VOICE. ALL RIGHT STUDIO, SETTLE DOWN. KEEP THE NOISE DOWN! TAKE FIVE, PLEASE— AND FIVE *MEANS* FIVE. NOBODY LEAVES THE FLOOR!

*(LORI NILSSON walks on, carrying a stool, her script, a cup of tea and a bulky paperback book. Red-haired and petite, SHE is dressed and made up as a sexy nightclub hostess. LORI is a stunner.*
*Settling on her canvas stool, SHE tries to be as inconspicuous as possible. PETER spots her.)*

PETER. (*Moves in.*) Hello, gorgeous. Having fun?

*(LORI regards him stonily, before answering; SHE seems to have no regard for his studio status, and PETER has to make all the going.)*

LORI. Fun? Yeah, I'm having fun—like when I go to the dentist.
PETER. Complaints?

LORI. Loafing around all the time, nobody knowing what's what—

PETER. You must be new to television.

LORI. Sure. Modelling's more my line. Just thought I'd give TV acting a whirl.

PETER. To see how the other half lives?

LORI. It's all experience. Care to sit down?

PETER. Do I look as though I need to?

LORI. (*Off-handedly.*) You're the star.

PETER. I won't argue with that.

*(LORI half-smiles and pretends to lose herself in her book. HE keeps his eyes on her.*

*A DRESSER, in a green overall with "BBC" embroidered in red on its top pocket, comes on carrying the grey trench-coat and tweed hat that are the trademarks of Peter's series. HE hands the great man a glass of Scotch-on-the-rocks.*

*PETER drinks, with his eyes on Lori. Then HE hands back the glass.)*

PETER. Fix me another and have it standing by on set. I'll be there directly.

*(The DRESSER nods, and withdraws as discreetly as he came.)*

LORI. (*Drily.*) I wouldn't take any bets.

PETER. Talking about stars—I play the Inspector, and that's it. Your part's just as important as mine, if the show's going to work.

LORI. (*Looks up.*) What's this then, "Be Kind To Extras" Day?

PETER. The name's Peter, didn't you know?

LORI. I know. Who doesn't?

*(Again SHE tries to settle to her reading. HE picks up the script SHE has dumped at the side of her stool and reads the name boldly scrawled across it.)*

PETER. "L.H. Nilsson"—with a double "s." Some sort of foreigner, are you?

LORI. Not exactly. The family came from Scandinavia, way back. "L" stands for Lorraine.

PETER. Pretty.

LORI. Friends call me Lori.

PETER. Does that include me?

LORI. If you like; I'm not particular. (*SHE tries to stick with her book.*)

PETER. That must be pretty gripping stuff. It wouldn't be Jeffrey Archer, by any chance?

LORI. Do me a favour. This is a serious scientific study.

PETER. Of what?

LORI. Astrology.

PETER. (*Succinctly.*) Cobbler's.

LORI. (*Closes the paperback and gazes at him.*) How was that again?

PETER. Sorry. You're from across the water, aren't you?

LORI. All the way from Grosse Point, Michigan.

PETER. I was trying to say horoscopes and all that sort of thing—codswallop—er—rubbish.

LORI. I might have expected that from you, Mr. Conway.

PETER. My friends call me Peter.

LORI. A closed mind, that's typical of November.

PETER. How d'you know my birth-sign? You must have read it somewhere.

LORI. Sorry to disappoint you, but it's written all over your face.

PETER. Starting where?

LORI. The eyes. Scorpio watches people all the time.

PETER. Not unless they're worth watching.

LORI. This book calls it "the eye of the devil."

PETER. Mine took years of practice to perfect—

LORI. Who're you kidding? You were born with that gimlet-gaze, mister, and probably scared the hell out of the midwife.

PETER. Tell me more.

LORI. (*Looks him up and down, pursing her lips.*) You're honest—but only in moderation. Loyal, too—but mostly to yourself and your own interests. You've got drive and ambition—boy, have you got ambition?—and you're as self-contained as a combination lock.

PETER. (*In close by this time.*) Is my particular lock worth picking?

LORI. Maybe. Scorpios are fascinating ... if not altogether likeable.

PETER. There's a difference?

LORI. To a sceptical Virgo, yes.

PETER. You mean I'm talking to a real, live Virgo?

LORI. *Astrologically* speaking. (*Point gained, SHE opens her paperback once more.*)

PETER. I'd like to go into this deeper, when we've got time: after the recording say, in my dressing-room?

LORI. If I read my charts right you're good and married.

PETER. Now that you *did* get from the Sunday papers.

LORI. I never read 'em—only the funnies. (*Looks up.*) When's *her* birthday?

PETER. June. She's Gemini.

LORI. Placid and long-suffering. Regrettably, cold at heart.

PETER. Watch it! That's my wife we're talking about!

LORI. But never underrate the Heavenly Twins: they only *seem* easy-going.

PETER. How about Virgo—easy-going enough for that goodnight drink?

LORI. I'm over here on a working visa, Mr. Conway, not open licence.

*(The TELEVISION VOICE booms again.)*

TV VOICE. STAND BY, STUDIO! ALL ON FOR THE NIGHT-CLUB SCENE, WE'RE READY TO *ROLL*!

*(LORI starts to gather her things together hastily.)*

PETER. Don't panic, they'll take hours yet.

LORI. I'm new here, remember? Fresh in from Modeltown. And I'm on at the beginning—

PETER. Break a leg.

LORI. Thank you—star!

PETER. Hey, how about that date?

LORI. Sorry, I have to go as soon as we finish.

PETER. Where to?

LORI. Brighton. I've got a little pad there—

PETER. Doing all right, aren't you, for five-and- a-half lines?

LORI. Daddy pays the bills.

PETER. And what does Daddy do, when he's not running the Bank of America?

LORI. (*Shrugs.*) He makes motor-cars. Do I get my script back?

PETER. Straight swop: one script, one Scotch-on- the-rocks?

LORI. (*Takes it.*) Okay, then—but not in your dressing-room. (*SHE scrambles off.*)

PETER. (*Calls out after her.*) Upstairs in the Club— you'll have three hundred chaperones! (*HE turns, and walks back to Drummond.*) I never thought she'd come, but she was there. Lori always keeps her word. It wasn't long before I knew the M23 like the back of my hand.

DRUMMOND. The Brighton motorway?

PETER. The road to freedom. And a certain amount of understanding. Lori turned out to be *my* brand of consolation: the only woman who still had any faith in me.

DRUMMOND. And then your wife found out. (*HE looks at the girl's picture again, before tucking it back in his pocket.*)

PETER. I didn't know she had—till you showed me that. Still, it rounds everything off nicely, don't you think?

DRUMMOND. (*Glances back, towards the stairs.*) Neglect, loneliness, and finally despair ... tell me the old, old story. (*Returns to notebook.*) We'll be needing this girl's particulars—

PETER. 41, Winchester Terrace; ground-floor flat.

DRUMMOND. Handy. Phone-number?

PETER. Brighton 68227. Can I ring and let her know what's going on?

DRUMMOND. I'd rather you waited, sir, till she's been interviewed.

PETER. You will—break it fairly gently?

DRUMMOND. I'm sure we can rely on the Brighton police to do that: they wear kid gloves I believe, down on the South Coast.

*(A KNOCK at the front door.)*

DRUMMOND. That'll be Forensic.

PETER. *(In some surprise.)* Forensic?

DRUMMOND. *(Starts for door.)* Nothing to worry about, sir—standard procedure. Oh, better leave everything just as we found it. *(HE replaces Peter's used glass behind the bar.)*

PETER. I wasn't aware that—

DRUMMOND. Just a tick, sir. *(Using his scarf to cover his hand again, HE switches off the lights.)*

*(The KNOCK is repeated sharply.)*

DRUMMOND. I'll let 'em in.

PETER. *(Commandingly.)* Sergeant Drummond!

DRUMMOND. *(Freezes on the spot.)* Sir?

PETER. Will that be all?

DRUMMOND. *(Tonelessly.)* Far as I'm concerned, sir: no further questions.

PETER. Right. Then get out of my mind.

*(THEME MUSIC SWELLS, then cuts off abruptly as:*
*Turning, PETER seizes both the curtains and flings them*
*wide.*
*Bright SUNLIGHT pours into the room.*
*DRUMMOND has vanished.*
*PETER looks round the room, smiling in private triumph.*
*LORI walks on from the bedroom as far as the landing,*
*where SHE pauses to do up buttons on the front of her*
*dress.)*

LORI. Okay, star?

PETER. Fine. I've just been going through it in my head.

LORI. Do you ever stop?

PETER. Not till it's all behind us.

*(HE meets her at the foot of the stairs and tries to kiss her,*
*but SHE holds his face away.)*

LORI. You'll call me as soon as you can?

PETER. Once we're in the clear. They may not let me do that, until you've been interviewed.

LORI. That's the scary bit.

PETER. You'll be great; and we've had plenty of rehearsal.

LORI. I'll be waiting at the flat all night. You will get through the minute you can?

PETER. (*Nodding.*) On that nice old-fashioned telephone you picked up at Harrods. The price you paid for that, it should be gold-plated!

LORI. It's heavy enough as it is. (*SHE pulls away from him to do her dress up tightly at the neck.*)

PETER. One for the road?

LORI. No more for me, thanks. (*Jerks her head at stairs.*) I remember what the last one did. Oh, let's not forget my glass.

PETER. I can look after that—

LORI. (*Going.*) My responsibility. And we did rehearse every detail, remember? (*SHE disappears in the direction of the bedroom.*)

(*PETER goes behind the bar and produces a whisky-decanter that until now has been hidden from view. It is about a quarter full. HE helps himself to a generous measure and drops ice into the drink.*

*LORI appears again with coat, handbag and her used glass, which SHE hands to him across the bar to be washed and put away.*)

LORI. All present and correct.

PETER. Where's the photograph?

LORI. (*Holds up bag.*) In here; it's not signed yet though.

PETER. Do that now.

(*LORI feels in her bag, and takes out a postcard photograph identical with the one DRUMMOND had on show. SHE holds it up for his inspection.*)

LORI. Okay professor?

PETER. Perfect. Sign it.

(*LORI turns to the desk to pick up something to write with.*)

PETER. Use your own pen.
LORI. Don't miss a trick, do you?
PETER. We can't afford to.

*(LORI gets a Papermate out of her handbag.*
*PETER comes away from the bar, bringing with him a*
*hand-towel. HE picks up the pen she has touched, wipes*
*it, and puts it back in place.)*

LORI. What shall I write?
PETER. Keep it simple.
LORI. You're not going to believe this, but I'm stuck
for words.
PETER. "With all my love." That'll do. Just sign it
"L."

*(LORI scribbles busily as HE watches, leaning over her to*
*kiss her neck.)*

LORI. (*Holds the picture up.*) Good enough?
PETER. I suppose that's just about decipherable.
LORI. I'd have you know I majored in English!
PETER. Don't worry, it doesn't show.

*(HE takes the photo from her, and crosses to put it in the*
*inside pocket of his sheepskin then HE returns the*
*towel to the bar, taking the opportunity to refresh his*
*drink, as LORI puts her personal pen away.)*

LORI. I looked up "scorpion" in the encyclopaedia, by
the way. And I quote—"A nocturnal arachnid that attacks

and paralyses its prey with a poison, injected by the long, curved tail. This is used for both defence and destruction."

PETER. I never knew I had one!

LORI. *(Soberly.)* "Its sting is sometimes fatal." *(SHE rises.)*

PETER. Sure you want to go through with it? No doubts, any more?

LORI. *(Positively.)* It's the only way there is to get what I want.

PETER. She'd never divorce me, although we could try—

LORI. I can't wait that long. Working visas have a limited life; and one thing I hate, it's long distance phone-calls. I want you on hand, star, and I want you permanently.

*(HE leaves his drink to come and put his arms around her.)*

PETER. Signed, sealed and delivered; with a band of gold.

LORI. You betcha. Daddy's Norwegian: that means he's kind of reactionary. He's not going to help with your future unless he's sure I have a vested interest. It comes of being a tycoon.

*(HE kisses her and for a moment SHE surrenders, before putting him at arm's length.)*

LORI. What time do you expect her back?

PETER. Not before six. And she never—ever—takes me by surprise.

LORI. (*Stroking his cheek.*) So what made us come downstairs in such a hurry?

PETER. I wanted time.

LORI. Time?

PETER. To run over it all again.

LORI. I have the whole thing off by heart.

PETER. This is the last chance we'll get; after that phone-call from my agent, it's got to be tonight.

LORI. You'll pick a quarrel first—about the job he offered?

PETER. Then I'll make sure it builds up into a flaming row.

*(HE sits on the settee and taps the place next to him. LORI joins him.)*

LORI. Which gives you good reason for storming out of here.

PETER. (*Nodding.*) And I come straight down to Brighton, by train—

LORI. Where we have a perfectly normal evening, driving out in my car along the coast and making contacts—

PETER. Check. We get back to your flat around midnight, and leave the Volvo in the garage with the garage-door unlocked.

LORI. I have the only key to the flat, and it stays in my possession.

PETER. And hang on to your car-keys, don't forget.

LORI. Sure, 'cos you'll be using duplicates. Then you take my car—

PETER. I drive up here, do what I have to do, and then drive back to Brighton. I'll have it washed on my way back, to clean off any London dirt. When you wake up in the morning, all you have to do is check the car.

LORI. You won't come in and let me know we made it?

PETER. No.

LORI. (*Seductively.*) I won't be all locked up, if you change your mind—

PETER. Not in daylight. Maybe you'd better run your Volvo down the road first thing—buy a sandwich, a magazine or something—

LORI. (*Puzzled.*) Why?

PETER. To get your fingerprints back on the steering-wheel.

LORI. You cover everything, don't you?

PETER. It's the only way, if it's going to work.

*(SHE rises quickly, taking a step away from him.)*

PETER. Losing your nerve?

LORI. No.

PETER. It's a challenge—

LORI. (*Softly.*) Only ... promise me ... there'll be no pain.

PETER. (*Rises and stands behind her.*) Repposal in alcohol? Safe, comfortable, and absolutely sure. All she has to do is take a couple of drinks. They don't even have to be doubles.

*(SHE turns to face him.)*

PETER. Back out now if you like; but no later.

LORI. *(Shakes head.)* This is what I want, star. It's something I've got to have. Only …

PETER. Only what?

LORI. I hope to God you never get your knife into me.

PETER. *(Reassuringly.)* No way. You and me: that's for keeps.

*(HE is on the point of taking her in his arms again but SHE moves away, ostensibly to get her coat.)*

LORI. I have to leave now. No more talking. Not in her house.

PETER. Go out the back and along the terrace.

LORI. Sneaking out like some cheap hooker? It never bothered you before.

PETER. It does today: the one time you can't be seen.

*(LORI holds his gaze for a moment, and it is clear SHE is totally infatuated with him.)*

LORI. You're mine—all mine. Between us, we're going to put you back where you belong.

PETER. I'll drink to that.

LORI. Hold me. Hold me very tight. Tell me you love me.

PETER. You know I do.

LORI. *Say it.*

PETER. I love you: I can't stop thinking about you.

*(THEY kiss, fervently.)*

LORI. Okay, I can do it. As long as I know that.

*(HE releases her tenderly, and SHE crosses to the windows. There SHE looks back at him for an instant.)*

LORI. See you. *(SHE slips out.)*

*(PETER's glance travels round the room. HE notices his car-coat still on the settee, and picks it up to return it to the cloaks cupboard.*

*HE must go upstairs now to make sure no traces remain there of Lori's afternoon visit.*

*Retrieving his drink, HE enjoys a sip of Scotch on the way. His whole manner is confident and relaxed, and there is no sign in it of urgency or even of concern.*

*As HE is mounting the stairs:)*

## QUICK CURTAIN

## Scene 2

*One hour later.*

*PETER is dozing on the settee as the door opens, and his WIFE enters.*

*This is the real-life STELLA ... warm, long-suffering, and understanding; but not in any way weak or indulgent.*

*The business suit SHE wears is smart although it is not expensive.*

STELLA. *(Closes door.)* Hi, Peter.

*(No response. SHE registers the whisky-decanter on the bar, and then makes for the stairs.)*

STELLA. Wake up, love—nearly tea time.

PETER. *(Opens his eyes.)* I wasn't asleep; just day-dreaming.

STELLA. You're doing too much of that lately.

PETER. Good for the soul. How d'it go?

STELLA. *(Pulls her hat off and shakes her hair free.)* Same as usual: nobody wants to know. *(SHE finds a cigarette at the desk and lights it up.)* There's no call for shorthand-typing any more. "Sorry, Mrs. Conway—are you familiar with computers?" Well, I'm not. I suppose I could take a course—but maybe I should lower my sights and find something different. Shopwork, perhaps—or maybe somebody needs a dim receptionist. I don't think I fancy cleaning, not just yet.

PETER. Now maybe you'll forget this charity assignment and settle—

STELLA. Don't call it that!

PETER. Can you find a better name? "Handout," for example?

STELLA. Most wives go out to work these days—

PETER. And the divorce-rate's one in four, isn't it; or has it climbed to three? I'd like this family to hang on to what little dignity it's got left—

STELLA. This *family*—?

*(Their eyes meet.)*

PETER. Thank God we never had any. One of the few wise decisions I ever made. (*HE goes to the whisky and fills up his glass.*)

STELLA. What makes you think we can afford luxuries like self-respect, while we're still paying for necessities like that?

PETER. (*Puts the decanter down again.*) One drink—one lousy drink!

STELLA. That thing was nearly full when I went out.

PETER. Haven't you noticed? The bottles get smaller as you get older—the same applies to decanters.

STELLA. (*Watches him drink.*) You realise … you're destroying yourself, bit by bit?

PETER. My health: my pigeon.

STELLA. Even if the agents came up with something worthwhile—

PETER. And it's my *career*! What's left of it.

STELLA. Have you eaten anything?

PETER. I don't think so, no. Lunchtime came—and went.

STELLA. It's your stomach too. You haven't been out, then?

PETER. Where the hell would I go?

STELLA. "One more try at the office" was what you said.

PETER. Give it a rest, lover. (*HE goes to fill up his glass.*)

STELLA. I'll make some coffee. Meanwhile, have another drink—lover.

(*SHE goes towards the kitchen.*)

PETER. Leave it.

STELLA. (*Halts.*) Sure. Whisky'll do fine, won't it?

PETER. You know what Richard would have said—in a brand-new old school tie—"Sorry old boy, nothing doing; not a god-damn thing. It's been a terrible year right across the board. And let's face it, you haven't got the clout you used to have."

STELLA. You don't have to accept that—

PETER. Makes you think though, doesn't it? What happens to poor bloody actors when television's finished with them? Talk about the slaughter of the innocents! (*HE swallows the drink down.*)

STELLA. It needn't have been like this

*(But PETER is on a favourite hobbyhorse now.)*

PETER. I was always the trusting type, you know: always believed everything I was told. Like Savage was only the beginning. Like doors would open up from then on. Even Zimmermann, the Big White Chief—*(Sneers.)*—lunches at the Caprice! (*HE refills his glass.*)

*(STELLA sighs, patiently. She has heard all this before.)*

PETER. We used to talk films and West End Theatre in those days; now I never even smell his cigar smoke. (*Mimics.*) "The Royal Shakespeare maybe, Peter ... even the National ..." Other telly-phonies had done it, why shouldn't I? Only it didn't work out like that, did it? Tell me, Mr. Zimmermann—whatever happened to Gala Night for Peter Conway?

*(Slight pause.)*

STELLA. It always takes you like this, doesn't it? When you're alone. It's like reading through an old diary—

PETER. So in answer to your question: no, I did not go to the office. I didn't even ring Richard.

STELLA. What else is new?

PETER. However, Richard rang me. With a great big wonderful offer no actor in his right mind could refuse. I'm wanted in Wardour Street tomorrow morning for discussions.

STELLA. *(Quickening.)* That could be a *film*—

PETER. It *is* a film.

STELLA. Darling, you never said!

PETER. A *commercial* film.

STELLA. *(Deflated.)* Oh.

PETER. You took the words right out of my mouth. *(HE drinks deeply.)*

STELLA. And that's a good enough reason, I suppose, for finishing off the whisky?

PETER. Can you think of a better?

STELLA. You won't even consider the offer?

PETER. *(Sits, nursing his glass.) What* offer—a whole string of crummy commercials? Cat-food. They want somebody for cat-food! *(HE takes another drink.)* The campaign's worth a fortune, and they're going spare looking for the right voice and personality. Rugged, but warm and sympatico with it. Some stupid prat with a deep voice and a homespun accent. "Able to work with animals, and possibly children." Possibly? The set'll be crawling with 'em.

STELLA. Won't you go this time—at least talk to them?

PETER. I'm an actor, not a bloody commercial traveller. You wouldn't understand.

STELLA. (*Stung.*) All right—act big—throw it in Richard's face!

PETER. I certainly will.

STELLA. He's only trying to *help*—

PETER. Is that what you're throwing in *my* face, the pair of you? What do you want—some kind of ventriloquists's dummy?

STELLA. We don't *care*—as long as it pays the bills.

PETER. I'm a pro. I've got *standards*. And I'm not lowering 'em for you, Richard—or any sodding cat-food manufacturer! (*HE empties what remains in the decanter into his glass.*)

STELLA. What standards are we talking about: two bottles a day?

PETER. Let's go on from there, shall we? Richard's known from the beginning how I feel about muck like this. So who encouraged him to throw it in *my* face—again?

STELLA. All I said was "Try it—see if Peter's changed his mind."

PETER. Well Peter hasn't. When *was* this, anyway—during one of your cosy little chats while my back was turned?

STELLA. We were going through the accounts the other day, for the umpteenth time. That man's got the patience of Job. Then he happened to suggest—

PETER. That you turn me into a block of wood with a talking head?

STELLA. (*Soft and intense.*) Will you—for God's sake—*stop acting*?

PETER. Having an agent who's gone off you's bad enough. But having a wife who sells you short behind your back—! And when the two of 'em start ganging up on you—

STELLA. Oh, go to hell!

PETER. I'm sure to: but I'll go there in my own way—

STELLA. The *professional* way?

PETER. Right: however many bottles it takes. (*HE drinks.*)

STELLA. I honestly believe that stuff's affecting your brain.

PETER. It never affected my work.

STELLA. You believe that, don't you? You honestly believe it. Don't you know—can't you *see*—that's why they won't offer you anything decent any more? It's because they can't! They daren't!

PETER. Don't stop there.

STELLA. *(Quietens.)* You were a good actor once—the best on their books. But you're not dependable any more—and that's what killed the series. Face it! It wasn't the planners, or the public—it was *you*, the famous Peter Conway. Too drunk, most of the time, to stand up and say the lines!

*(Long pause.)*

PETER. Thanks a bunch. (*HE drains his drink, puts the glass down, and gets his coat.*)

STELLA. Don't go off again. Sit down and *listen* for once—

PETER. I've heard all I want.

STELLA. All right, have it your way! But before you go, hear this. I won't try and stop you tonight, because this isn't like all the other nights. This is new; it's different.

PETER. (*Goading her.*) Tell me more.

STELLA. Go now and it's final. There'll be no coming back this time, I'll make damned sure of that.

PETER. With a little help from your friends?

STELLA. I mean it—*mean* it, Peter.

PETER. You're a big girl now—haven't you learned? Never kick a man when he's down. Especially a husband. He's liable to turn round and kick back—hard. (*Wrenches door open.*) I don't know when I'll be back.

STELLA. (*Breaks.*) Who bloody well cares?

*(HE slams out.*

*SHE looks after him for an instant, then sits at the desk and lights a cigarette, collecting herself. SHE picks up the phone and dials.)*

STELLA. Richard? It's Stella. I've made up my mind, and I'm going through with it. (*SHE draws in smoke.*) Absolutely sure. Come round tonight and we'll make all the arrangements. Peter won't be here: he's just gone out and won't be back till late. (*Her mouth twists.*) Because I know *Peter.* (*Slight pause.*) Capable? Of course I'm capable. He's been asking for this for a long time; now he's going to get it. (*SHE hangs up. Her glance falls on the framed photograph of her husband which stands on the desk, matching her own. SHE picks it up and studies his features for a long moment, shaking her head slowly from side to side. Suddenly SHE smashes it against the corner of the desk—and hurls the remains away from her in contempt.)*

**CURTAIN**

## ACT II

### Scene 1

*After midnight.*

*The curtains are fully drawn and the room is in DIM LIGHT. One of the armchairs has been turned to face upstage.*

*STELLA comes in from out of doors.*

*Closing the front door behind her, SHE switches on soft LIGHTING. SHE looks pale and drawn; and her manner is preoccupied, as if she is in a world of her own that will suffer no intrusion.*

*As SHE moves towards the stairs a FIGURE rises out of the armchair and faces her. STELLA pulls up with a gasp—before realising it is her husband.*

STELLA. It's late.
PETER. *Too* late?
STELLA. What do you want?
PETER. You.

*(Pause.)*

STELLA. It is too late, Peter. Far too late.
PETER. Let's talk.
STELLA. Talking's easy. Doing things, that's the hard part. Making decisions, and sticking to them—(*SHE breaks off.*)

55

PETER. What's the matter?

STELLA. I feel—lost, somehow. Lost and lonely. I think I must be very tired.

PETER. What you need's a drink.

STELLA. No. Why did you draw the curtains? (*SHE crosses to pull one of them back, and open a window; SHE stands, breathing in cold night air to brace herself.*) You know I can't bear to be shut in.

PETER. Where've you been till now?

STELLA. Driving. A long drive. Trying to make sense out of my life—finally.

PETER. Alone?

STELLA. Richard was with me earlier. We've been out looking for you in all the usual places. When we couldn't find you, he went home.

PETER. (*Moves towards her, trying to establish some of the old rapport.*) I know what you expected. Peter Conway, back in the old routine. Clubs ... bars ... then police stations and casualty wards. How are they all, the old familiar faces?

STELLA. The same as ever.

PETER. Remember that bastard at Hammersmith? (*Laughs mirthlessly.*) Duty sergeant. Took all my clothes away and left me freezing in my underpants all night. Stone-cold cell: bucket in the corner. Then he had the nerve to come in at sparrow-fart with a teabag in a cracked cup, and ask me to send his wife a signed photograph!

STELLA. Please go. I've got to be by myself.

PETER. (*Moves in closer.*) I *need* you—

STELLA. Don't come near me.

PETER. Come away from the window. The weather's treacherous at this time of year.

*(Uncaring, STELLA crosses to the settee, where SHE shrugs off her coat to leave it on the arm.*
*Behind her back, PETER shuts the window and draws the curtains close.)*

PETER. Let's talk, I said.

STELLA. There's nothing left to talk about.

PETER. One drink. Five minutes. That's not too much to ask surely, after ten whole years?

*(STELLA is helping herself to a cigarette at the desk.*
*HE crosses to where the whisky-decanter stands, now half-full, at the bar. There HE pours out generous measures for them both.)*

PETER. After that … if you still feel the same, I'll go. That's a promise.

*(No answer. HE brings the whisky.)*

PETER. Just let me say I'm sorry. That's all I'm here for, to apologise. Sorry for all the hurt I've brought into your life.

*(STELLA takes her glass and sits, without making any attempt to drink.)*

PETER. I'm sorry for the mess I've made of things and sorry for what it's done to you. Sorry for being me: a small-time actor who had one lucky break and let it go straight to his head. Big man ... small finish. (*HE watches her for a moment.*)

STELLA. Take my advice, you'll go away. Tonight. Go far away, and stay there.

PETER. Why are you trembling?

(*Silently, STELLA studies her glass.*)

STELLA. (*Murmurs.*) Oh, what's the difference?

(*SHE takes a drink.
This encourages HIM to sit next to her.*)

PETER. I can change, Stella—I will change.

(*STELLA sips again, in silence.*)

PETER. One more try. Just one. (*Leans in closer.*) We'll do everything you say, all the things you've planned. I'll work like stink—at anything—starting with that interview in the morning. I'll nail that job! It's a whole string of commercials, enough to put us back on our feet again.

STELLA. (*Finishes her drink, before turning to look him in the face.*) Doesn't she want you any more?

PETER. Who?

STELLA. The girl in Brighton. That's where you've come from, isn't it?

(*PETER frowns.*)

STELLA. They're all the same, aren't they, the—stand-ins? They lie, they cheat, they steal. But when it comes to the crunch not one of 'em's ready to take full responsibility. Because, ultimately, no woman wants your kind of total dependence. It stinks.

PETER. What's all this about Brighton?

STELLA. Lori. Sexy little Lori from Grosse Point, Michigan. She's got all the money in the world, they tell me; enough to buy her anything she wants. What do you fancy, Peter? A new start—abroad—or a brand-new career right here in London? Which is it to be?

PETER. What's got into you?

STELLA. She wasn't the first, was she? That was an over-sexed little secretary, who wanted to be an actress. You helped her into a flat in Holland Park, but it didn't last long. (*SHE begins to tremble again, as SHE recounts his exploits.*) Then there was that French director's wife, Michelle. It drove him out of television, didn't it? And very nearly out of his mind. After that the young blonde bitch who played your sister in the series ... Do I have to go on?

PETER. I didn't realise I was being watched—

STELLA. You're not; not any more. I paid the man off when I realised Lori was something special—something else again, in your terms.

PETER. And in yours?

STELLA. Something dangerous. Something with which I was no longer willing to compete.

PETER. (*Takes her glass and refills it at the bar.*) I'm glad it's all out in the open. You might as well know I finished with Lori tonight, down in Brighton. From now on it's you and me—exclusive. (*HE holds her glass out.*)

STELLA. No more.

PETER. One for the road; if it has to be.

STELLA. (*Takes the whisky HE offers, and studies it.*) Richard said you'd do this. He knew you'd come crawling back: I only thought you might. Neither of us guessed it would be quite so soon.

PETER. What the hell would Richard know?

STELLA. More than you think. He also said I'd always take you back; but he was wrong there.

PETER. Let him be right, for one last time.

STELLA. That wouldn't suit him. You see, he's declared a personal interest—he wants us to go away together. (*SHE drinks.*)

PETER. You—and Richard?

STELLA. You didn't even suspect. But that's you, isn't it, Peter? (*SHE rises, drains her glass, and sets it down positively.*) We've had the drink. We've talked. Now get out.

(*SHE moves to get her coat, touching the pockets and looking round the settee. HE doesn't move.*)

PETER. Looking for something?

STELLA. My gloves. I must have left them somewhere. It doesn't matter. (*SHE goes off up the stairs.*)

(*PETER takes off his car-coat and lays it to one side. Then HE picks up her empty glass and pours his own drink into it. HE goes behind the bar, rinses his used glass, and puts it carefully away.*

*As HE moves towards the stairs, something makes him stop and glance over at the hi-fi.*)

*HE crosses to the installation and flicks a cassette out of the cabinet. It has recently been played. After checking the label HE smiles to himself, before putting the tape back in place and switching it on.*

*THEME MUSIC swells.*

*PETER seats himself comfortably, as if to enjoy the music.*

*STELLA reappears on the landing. SHE has changed into a housecoat.)*

STELLA. Switch that off.

PETER. (*Without moving.*) The theme from "Inspector Savage"—disturbing, but very appropriate.

STELLA. (*Stands, humiliated.*) You're not being honest: especially with yourself.

PETER. Were you being honest just now? If so, why have you been playing it?

STELLA. I listened to the tape this afternoon. For the last time.

PETER. I'll leave as soon as it ends. (*HE rises, picks up her glass, and moves towards her.*)

STELLA. (*Lunges quickly towards the hi-fi.*) I said turn the damned thing off! (*SHE flicks the switch herself, and the noise cuts out.*)

*(The PHONE goes sharply.)*

STELLA. *(Puts a hand to her head, as if unable to bear the ringing.)* You take it.

PETER. No, thanks. We'll ignore it.

*(SHE watches the phone, as it continues to ring; then SHE forces herself to go and answer it.)*

PETER. Whoever it is, I'm not here.

STELLA. *(Picks up receiver.)* Yes? Hello, Richard. No, he's not. My husband isn't expected and he isn't wanted. I'm fine—but I badly need rest. Do that if you like, and don't worry. Goodnight. *(SHE hangs up.)* Why wasn't I supposed to answer it?

PETER. I've got some pride left. Not much, but enough to make me hate the idea of anyone crowing over me—especially Richard.

STELLA. You said you weren't here before I picked up the phone.

PETER. It had to be him, after what you told me.

STELLA. You said you weren't here *whoever it was.*

PETER. I had reasons.

STELLA. You always have. Because *(As SHE works it out.)* you're not supposed to be in London, are you? You're supposed to be in Brighton—with your whore.

PETER. Don't call her that!

*(SHE turns to pick up her drink.)*

PETER. Look, why can't you accept—

STELLA. Where did this come from? We'd run out of whisky.

PETER. I brought some with me.

STELLA. *(Crosses slowly to the bar.)* You bought Scotch. You brought it here. Then you poured it in the decanter, and put it behind the bar?

PETER. Can you think of a better place?

STELLA. At this hour of night? And knowing you might not be staying?

PETER. You've never turned me out before.

STELLA. There's never been a "before" like this. (*SHE faces him across the bar.*) I've only had two drinks, but they were large ones. Large enough, would you say?

PETER. I don't know what you're getting at.

STELLA. (*Picks up decanter.*) This. The real reason you came back. To eliminate me. (*SHE pours all the Scotch down the sink, followed by the contents of her glass. Then SHE comes away from the bar and returns to him.*)

PETER. Now what … the police?

STELLA. Now nothing: there's no need. (*SHE is swaying visibly, but seems determined to stay on her feet. Feeling in the pocket of her housecoat, SHE produces a small phial and holds it out to him.*) Do you know what this is?

PETER. Repposal. Yours.

*(SHE turns it upside-down: the phial is empty. HER voice begins to slur.)*

STELLA. I took every single one I had—upstairs, just now. That's all I came back for. (*SHE tosses it at his feet.*) You could have saved yourself the trouble. (*SHE turns away from him, to make for the stairs ... but SHE is by now too weak to reach them. With a harsh, rasping cry, SHE collapses against the hand-rail.*)

PETER. Stella!

*(HE starts forward involuntarily and then stops to watch, fascinated, as SHE crumples to the ground.*

*STELLA lies still.*

*HE forces himself to cross to her. HE feels her heart. Then HE backs slowly away from her.*

*Gathering speed, PETER goes to his coat and takes out his driving-gloves. HE scans the room, as HE slips them on. Then HE picks up the empty phial from the carpet and takes it to the desk. Going to the bar, HE gets the decanter and Stella's used glass, and places these next to the phial. From his coat HE takes the prepared photograph of Lori, and sets it down with the other evidence he has assembled.*

*As HE returns to Stella, his actions are slowing again. HE draws his fingers over her brow, closing her eyes. Only then is HE ready to slip off the gold ring SHE wears.*

*HE looks down at her body with their wedding ring in his hand.*

*Then he bends to pick Stella up and carry her off to the bedroom.*

*As HE straightens, holding his dead wife in his arms:)*


## QUICK  CURTAIN


### Scene  2

*Saturday morning.*
*The room is immaculate, and the curtains are open wide.*
*Drummond's scarf is spread over the armchair.*

*PETER sits alone, staring at it.*

*DRUMMOND comes down from upstairs, studying his notes. HE is an older man than we met earlier on—and is now grizzled and mature, with no illusions left, either about his job or life in general. His hair is greying, and these days HE has to resort to the occasional use of a pair of rimless glasses. HE has these on now.*

DRUMMOND. How're you feeling, sir?

PETER. I'll be okay.

DRUMMOND. It must have been a heck of a shock. (*Glances round briefly.*) Didn't leave much mess did they, Forensic?

PETER. No. They were very considerate.

DRUMMOND. Everything's back to normal in the bedroom. There won't be much for your charlady to do this morning.

PETER. We don't have cleaners any more. Stella—used to take care of all that sort of thing.

DRUMMOND. One of our rules, that is: always leave a place as tidy as you find it, wherever it happens to be. I've written out a receipt for the wedding ring. I'll be taking that with me—

PETER. Of course.

*(DRUMMOND holds out a piece of paper, but his offer is ignored. HE leaves it on the desk, and checks on his inside pocket.)*

DRUMMOND. Now then, that girl's picture. *(Finds it.)* Yes, got it here. I think that about does it, sir. (*HE tucks his notebook and the photograph away.*)

PETER. (*Forces himself to make ordinary conversation.*) You're a much older man than I remembered.

DRUMMOND. We go grey young in the police force.

PETER. How's your wife these days?

DRUMMOND. Old Rentamouth? Same as usual.

PETER. Still watches television, does she?

DRUMMOND. Not so much nowadays, I'm happy to say. Me, I never watch the telly—never. Look at Coronation Street last night: what a load o' rubbish.

PETER. How about the police series?

DRUMMOND. (*Pained.*) Leave it out, sir! Television coppers? I wouldn't pay 'em out in buttons.

PETER. You used to like Inspector Savage—

DRUMMOND. No, that was the wife. I only came across it once or twice. I've seen worse. And— (*Grinning.*)—actors have to make a living, I suppose.

PETER. Sometimes I wonder why.

(*A discreet TOOT comes from a motor vehicle outside.*)

DRUMMOND. They're ready for you.

PETER. I suppose it's absolutely necessary for me to go along?

DRUMMOND. Formal identification, sir? Essential. It shouldn't take long.

PETER. I hope not. (*HE crosses to get his coat out of the cupboard.*)

DRUMMOND. I could fix for you to ride in the doctor's car if you prefer—

PETER. What's it like outside—many people about?

DRUMMOND. Street's full to bursting. Ambulance and sirens blaring, it always draws the crowds.

PETER. And besides, everybody knows who lives here.

DRUMMOND. Pardon?

PETER. Any Press out there?

DRUMMOND. Couldn't say, sir. I didn't notice any ratbags.

PETER. They will be.

DRUMMOND. Tell you what, you follow on in a few minutes when the ambulance has gone. I'll have a squad car standing by.

PETER. Thanks very much.

*(HE lays the coat down again as DRUMMOND makes for the door.)*

DRUMMOND. All part of the service.

PETER. By the way, has anybody been in touch with Brighton yet?

DRUMMOND. I haven't heard; I'll give Control a buzz while I'm out there.

PETER. It's extraordinary. (*Fishing.*) We've talked so much about the girl, yet probably you'll never even meet her.

DRUMMOND. Stranger things have happened.

PETER. Surely they're capable of taking a simple statement down in Brighton?

DRUMMOND. Just about. But this is our case, isn't it? Metropolitan.

PETER. It's your *enquiry*, certainly.

DRUMMOND. So I might just have the odd word with her, if there's time.

*(The HORN sounds again.)*

DRUMMOND. 'Scuse me. *(HE goes out.)*

*(The latch on the front door has been left up, for ease of entry and exit during the police examination of the premises.*
*PETER goes to the telephone and dials Lori's number. HE has to wait, and is even then frustrated.*
*HE clamps his hand down on the hook in annoyance. Then HE dials again, and listens carefully.)*

PETER. Damn and blast!

*(HE rams the phone down irritably and is turning away from it, when his glance falls on the striped scarf that Drummond has left behind.*
*HE picks this up and muses on it for a moment. Then HE slings it round his neck and strides D.R.*
*THEME MUSIC.*
*PETER opens the concealed door D.R., to reveal a green-painted corridor backing with police posters on it.*
*His whole manner changes now as HE assumes the role of DET. SERGEANT DRUMMOND, conducting an imaginary cross-examination in the interview room at a Brighton police station.)*

PETER. Come in, please. Ready for you now.
LORI. *(Enters, in a cold fury.)* What does a person have to do to get attention round here—a full frontal?

PETER. (*Offers her a chair, politely.*) M o s t interviewees prefer to talk sitting down.

LORI. Not me! Still, after all that hanging around— (*SHE grabs it, and plonks herself unceremoniously down.*) Okay if I smoke?

PETER. There's no law against it—yet.

LORI. Fine! (*LIGHTS up.*) Just who are you, mister?

PETER. Drummond. Bill Drummond. Detective-sergeant, Metropolitan Police.

LORI. So I'm impressed. What are you doing so far away from home?

PETER. Investigating what might be called a case of suicide.

LORI. And that's why I've been kept in that deep freeze out there—just waiting around until you got here?

PETER. Englishmen always take their time, miss— you have to, with the sort of cars we've got. Besides, the Brighton bobbies had one or two things to check on, before you and I could talk.

LORI. What kind of things?

PETER. Nothing to worry about: what we call standard procedure.

LORI. I call it nerve! Would you mind telling me what the hell I'm doing here?

PETER. You're assisting the police in their enquiries.

LORI. Bullshit!

PETER. (*Patiently.*) Now about this friend of yours Mr. Conway—

LORI. I told those two stumblebums who brought me here—

PETER. (*Finishes it for her.*) I know. That he'd been at your flat in Winchester Terrace all night long.

LORI. Right on! He went off at the crack of dawn to keep some stupid appointment. (*Well-rehearsed in this part.*) I haven't seen or heard from him since.

PETER. Are you sure?

LORI. Maybe I should do the video, the number of times I've said that!

PETER. Would you be willing to say it again, in a witness-box?

LORI. If that'll make everybody happy—sure!

PETER. I wouldn't be too eager, if I were you.

LORI. How come? What's Peter supposed to have done?

PETER. (*Calmly.*) Murder.

LORI. (*Stares at him.*) Where do you get these cute little jokes of yours—at play-school? (*SHE starts to rise.*)

PETER. Sit down, little girl. Let's remember two things, shall we? I don't like bad language, and I can't stand insults—especially from beginners. Take my advice: sit back, shut up, and pay attention.

LORI. To what?

PETER. To how Peter Conway hoped to get away with it.

LORI. (*Sits down again.*) Okay, sergeant—but you'd better remember something, too: all you're entitled to from me is a simple statement.

PETER. That's all we want.

*(HE spreads his hands, innocently.
LORI answers this with a glare.)*

LORI. Anything else—like question and answer, and where were you on the night of June the third?—I want a lawyer here, and I want him fast.

PETER. But nobody's accusing *you* of anything, are they? Not even accessory to the fact. Not yet.

LORI. I know nothing: I say nothing.

PETER. That suits me fine: just concentrate on listening.

*(HE starts to move around, working up quite a pace as HE tells his story.*
*We are now watching a good actor, as HE directs himself in a first-class performance.)*

PETER. Once upon a time, there was a famous television star whose marriage had gone well and truly on the rocks. Who needed a little encouragement—if not actual support—from somebody younger than his wife. And who wanted it urgently. So yesterday he took action. After a flaming row with his missus Peter Conway did a runner, and caught the 6:28 from Victoria.

LORI. You know the train?

PETER. He made sure of it, by picking a row with the guard and supplying his name and address.

LORI. Everybody knows Peter, he's a star.

PETER. D'you mind, miss? You're breaking the rules. Your friend checked into Brighton at 7:37, and he was with you from then on. From eight o'clock till midnight it was party-time.

LORI. Is that indictable?

PETER. The pair of you drove out along the coast to dine and dance, leaving plenty of reminders wherever you

called. Then it was back to your flat, where you played
tapes and CDs till after midnight. (*HE helps himself to a
cigarette. The brand is Drummond's.*) Sometime after that,
Peter sneaked out on his own, to where you'd left your
garage closed but not locked. Soon he was on his way to
Chelsea, with nobody any the wiser. In your car.

*(HE blows smoke out as, smiling impudently, LORI takes
a set of car-keys out of her bag.)*

LORI. Without these?
PETER. He used duplicates.
LORI. Where are they now?
PETER. Probably in some rubbish bin between here
and London. Where we'll never find 'em, anyway.

*(LORI tucks the keys away again, her confidence totally
unshaken.)*

LORI. Before you spell it out, that means I must have
been in on the deal. Therefore, hadn't you better warn me?
PETER. That won't be necessary.
LORI. How come?
PETER. You're not talking, are you? You're just
listening. Up in London, Peter dealt with Mrs. Conway in
his own sweet way and left everything looking like suicide.
He brought your car back, closed the garage door and
dropped the latch. He walked to the station and caught the
7:56, took a cab from Victoria and strolled in home just
after nine o'clock. Bingo!
LORI. And then what?

PETER. After discovering the body—which can't have come as much of a surprise—he rang a doctor and then got in touch with us. End of story.

*(All this leaves LORI shaken, but still under control.)*

LORI. That's your version?

PETER. That's what happened.

LORI. And now, so you get to win a silver star, where's the proof?

PETER. That's where you come in—if you know what's good for you.

LORI. Like I said before, no comment.

PETER. Wake up, Lori! Stop thinking about his future and start worrying about your own.

LORI. *(Rises.)* All right—school's out!

PETER. *(Confronts her.)* What's it all in aid of, eh? A lush, a deadbeat! We've been pulling the wraps off this pin-up boy of yours all morning. You know he's headed for bankruptcy, or didn't he mention that?

LORI. It's not important—

PETER. It is to him—vital! And he's been in trouble with us before, did you know that? Drunk and disorderly, dangerous driving, breach of the peace. You name it, and Peter Conway's had a go.

LORI. I won't hear a word against him—

PETER. Of course not! 'Cos you're the reforming type, aren't you? You're going to make something out of him— big deal! What with you, and fifty thousand pounds of insurance money, he's sitting pretty.

LORI. That's way out of line—

PETER. Only one thing stood in the way, didn't it? His wife.

LORI. (*Heatedly.*) He loves *me*!

PETER. He loved Stella once—and look what happened to her.

LORI. She couldn't hold him!

PETER. She did her best, for ten long bloody years!

LORI. And then she lost out, so she took too many pills! That doesn't prove he killed her—(*SHE pulls up short.*)

PETER. How did you come to know that, little girl—*about the pills*?

LORI. (*Has frozen.*) You said she—

PETER. (*Shaking his head.*) No I didn't.

LORI. They told me she'd opted out when they picked me up.

PETER. I doubt that, since they were under strict instructions—

LORI. No, I remember now! Peter phoned me as soon as he found the body—(*Again SHE stops.*)

PETER. I thought there'd been no communication between you since he left Brighton?

LORI. I was lying—

PETER. (*Cracks down.*) You're lying now! Let's have the truth.

LORI. (*Stares at him, beaten, then her head drops on her chest.*) What the hell am I going to do?

PETER. The whole truth, and nothing but the truth.

LORI. You win. He planned it all, for the two of us. I gave him the use of my car, and did everything he said.

PETER. (*Strides D.R.*) We'll have that down on paper—(*Opens door.*)—there's a shorthand-writer waiting.

LORI. Had it all worked out, didn't you?
PETER. All part of the service.
LORI. England—!

*(Despondently SHE makes her way out, and PETER closes the door behind her.*
*HE now walks back towards the desk, pausing only to pull off Drummond's scarf and leave it exactly where he found it.*
*HE sits at the phone and is about to try it once more, when there is a perfunctory KNOCK at the front door and DRUMMOND enters.)*

DRUMMOND. There you go, sir. The ambulance is off, and there's a squad-car at the end of the terrace, waiting for you.

PETER. (*Picks up his coat and starts for the windows—then HE pauses.*) Aren't you coming?

DRUMMOND. I'll hang on here, if you don't mind.

PETER. Why?

DRUMMOND. (*Mildly.*) There might just be the odd phone-call.

*(PETER's glance shoots to the phone, then HE looks straight at Drummond.)*

PETER. Have they contacted the girl yet?

DRUMMOND. I believe the Brighton police picked her up an hour ago; she's with them now.

PETER. I warn you, if they try any rough stuff—

DRUMMOND. Why should they? With us, violence is a last resort. (*Grins.*) We leave all that to the telly, sir—no offence.

(*PETER gives him a hard look, and then goes out and along the terrace.*
*DRUMMOND now has work to do.*
*Going behind the bar, HE looks all round it carefully, checking on shelves that are out of our view.*
*Apparently HE is unable to find what he is looking for. HE turns the tap on and lets it run, listening to it pensively. Then HE turns it off again, leaves the bar, crosses to the desk, and dials a number.*)

DRUMMOND. Bill Drummond—I'm still on the scene. What's the good word from the South Coast? (*Pause.*) Pity. Get on to 'em again, will you? Ask 'em to cover all Conway's movements while he was down there: check and double-check. I want names, times, eye-witnesses. Incidentally, they were swanning round in the girl's car last night; I want that gone over from top to bottom. I know I'm fussy—that's why I'm still a sergeant.

(*A KNOCK at the front door.*)

DRUMMOND. (*Still on phone.*) Oh, that. Yes, take her prints; and keep in touch. (*HE hangs up, and goes to answer the door.*)
RICHARD. (*Off.*) Good morning. My name's Richard Shaw.
DRUMMOND. Good of you to come round, sir. (*HE opens the door wide.*)

*(RICHARD enters. HE is well-groomed, quiet and reserved. It is plain HE feels the loss of STELLA deeply.)*

RICHARD. Thank you.

DRUMMOND. *(Closes door.)* I'm Detective-sergeant Drummond, in charge of the case.

RICHARD. Detective? *(Frowns.)* May I have a word with my client, please?

DRUMMOND. I'm sorry, Mr. Conway's out on important business.

RICHARD. *(Guesses.)* The identification?

DRUMMOND. Yes; he won't be long. Before he comes back, I'd like a quiet word with you.

*(RICHARD stays silent, as the POLICEMAN takes out his notebook.)*

DRUMMOND. According to our information, sir, you were the last person to see Mrs. Conway alive.

RICHARD. I suppose I must have been.

DRUMMOND. When the husband rang you to break the news, you said you'd been out with her till the early hours of this morning?

RICHARD. Correct.

DRUMMOND. And he found the body himself, just after nine o'clock. *(Takes out cigarette-packet.)* Smoke?

RICHARD. I don't, thanks.

DRUMMOND. Me, I'm hooked; it's what you might call an occupational hazard. Please sit down.

*(RICHARD takes a seat, as DRUMMOND lights up.)*

DRUMMOND. Thought a lot about Mrs. Conway, didn't you?

RICHARD. Everyone did.

DRUMMOND. Yes, but you in particular. Over and above the line of duty, would you say?

RICHARD. That's a very personal question.

DRUMMOND. Suicide's a very personal matter. Murder's even more so.

*(Pause.)*

RICHARD. You can't be serious.

DRUMMOND. I never joke, sir, not about serious crime.

RICHARD. *(Quietly.)* God Almighty. *(HE gets out of his seat and crosses to the windows, to stare out.)*

DRUMMOND. Let's repeat the question. How fond, Mr. Shaw?

RICHARD. Do you know who, or why?

DRUMMOND. We'll get to that, sir; one thing at a time.

RICHARD. If you want to know—*(Turning.)*—I'd have married Stella tomorrow. I've asked her to leave her husband half a dozen times.

DRUMMOND. Even though he was a close friend of yours?

RICHARD. Once. Now he's just a client; and not a very important one at that.

DRUMMOND. Thank you for coming out with it. It's only fair to tell you, your client's been equally frank. What exactly happened here last night, from your point of view?

RICHARD. (*Moves back to his chair.*) Stella rang me after he'd walked out on her. You know about that?

DRUMMOND. He told us.

RICHARD. (*Sits again.*) I came round here and we talked. She said this time it was final, she'd had enough. I had to insist that we go out and look for him.

DRUMMOND. Just when things were going your way?

RICHARD. You didn't know Stella. Not the real Stella. Good, bad, or indifferent, she loved him. She'd never have left him while he was down on his luck. If I wanted her—and, my God, I did—my only chance was to change that luck somehow.

DRUMMOND. (*Cottons on.*) The appointment?

RICHARD. (*Nods.*) That contract was worth nearly a hundred thousand pounds. Enough to pay all his debts, and put Peter Conway back on velvet.

DRUMMOND. And he came home this morning to keep the appointment of his own accord.

RICHARD. I wasn't to know he would. The last time Peter crashed out of here, it took more than two weeks to locate him. When we did, we pulled him out of a ward for alcoholics—more dead than alive.

DRUMMOND. I'd heard he was a drinker, but I'd no idea it was that bad. Was Mrs. Conway similarly afflicted?

RICHARD. No.

DRUMMOND. It's a disease, you know; and sometimes catching.

RICHARD. Stella was altogether different from the man she married: she had twice his backbone.

DRUMMOND. Did she drink much while the two of you were out?

RICHARD. Soft drinks only. We had a job to do.

DRUMMOND. And when it failed?

RICHARD. I brought her back at half past eleven, quarter to twelve.

DRUMMOND. You can't be more accurate?

RICHARD. Is it important?

DRUMMOND. Anything could be; we're dealing with sudden death, sir.

RICHARD. I know I got home at twelve-thirty, but I had to hunt for a cab after leaving here.

DRUMMOND. You'd been out in the Porsche then, not in your own car?

RICHARD. We used taxis. They still know where to park in the West End.

DRUMMOND. Why didn't you use the same cab that brought you back?

RICHARD. We'd walked the last hundred yards or so, along the Embankment. After the sort of night we'd had, we both felt like a breath of fresh air.

DRUMMOND. So you left the lady on her doorstep before midnight. She didn't think to ask you in for a nightcap?

RICHARD. Yes, but I didn't feel like one. And I had the perfect excuse: I drink Scotch, and Stella said they'd run out.

DRUMMOND. Was that unusual?

RICHARD. Very. Apparently, Peter finished the last bottle before he left.

*(Slight pause.)*

DRUMMOND That's all you can tell us?

RICHARD. Not quite. I was restless when I got home, unsettled, too much on my brain. I didn't feel like going to bed and couldn't sleep when I did. Finally I rang her up at three o'clock this morning to ask if he'd come back; but mainly, to find out how she was. She'd seemed strange—detached, sort of—all evening.

DRUMMOND. How did she seem on the phone?

RICHARD. Perfectly normal; but she admitted she was very tired. She was on her way to bed, and told me not to worry.

DRUMMOND. She didn't give any sign that she had suicide in mind?

RICHARD. None whatever. D'you think I'd have hung up, if she had? She asked me to call her again this morning.

DRUMMOND. Did she? (*Leaning forward.*) You're sure that was her suggestion?

RICHARD. No, wait. I said I would, and she said "Do that," something of the sort. I felt better afterwards, much more relaxed. I took a tablet and went straight to sleep.

DRUMMOND. Repposal?

RICHARD. I beg your pardon?

DRUMMOND. The name of the tablet, sir—Repposal?

RICHARD. (*Nods.*) How did you guess?

DRUMMOND. Mr. Conway told us you recommended them to her in the first place.

(*Another slight pause.*)

RICHARD. How do you suppose that makes me feel… now?

*(Their conversation is interrupted by PETER, who walks swiftly along the terrace and into the room. HE pulls up short on seeing Richard.)*

PETER. What's going on?

RICHARD. 'Morning, Peter.

PETER. I asked you not to come.

RICHARD. *(Nods towards Drummond.)* They had other ideas.

PETER. Sergeant?

DRUMMOND. *(Explains.)* As a material witness, Mr. Shaw was the last person to see the deceased alive.

PETER. That's different.

DRUMMOND. As far as we know.

PETER. *(Throws him a glance and then moves over to the bar, dragging off his coat.)* Anyone like a drink— Richard?

RICHARD. No, thanks.

PETER. *(Pours himself a large brandy.)* Brandy, sergeant?

DRUMMOND. Not just now, thank you.

PETER. Sod you both. I've earned mine. *(HE takes a hefty swig.)*

DRUMMOND. Mr. Shaw, I wonder if you'd mind going round to the station, so's we can get all this down on paper?

RICHARD. I'd prefer to have a word with my client first; in private.

DRUMMOND. I'm sure that'll come. Meanwhile—

PETER. *(To Richard.)* Do as he says. I need to be on my own for a bit.

DRUMMOND. Mr. Conway's had quite a morning: finger-prints, photographers, the full treatment.

RICHARD. I understand. (*Turns to Peter.*) Anyway, you know what I want to say.

PETER. Yes. Thanks. (*HE finishes his drink.*)

(*DRUMMOND has slung his scarf around his neck.*)

DRUMMOND. This way, sir.

PETER. Did you have any luck, sergeant—while I was out?

DRUMMOND. Luck?

PETER. (*Reminds him.*) The odd phone-call?

DRUMMOND. (*Somehow relieved.*) Ah, I see what you mean! No, nobody rang. It's been as quiet as the grave round here—if you'll pardon the phrase. (*HE goes out.*)

RICHARD. Look, Peter—

PETER. Not now. Nothing now. I'll ring you.

RICHARD. Do that. This afternoon. (*HE follows DRUMMOND out, closing the door behind him.*)

(*PETER waits for a second and then goes to it and drops the latch.*

*HE returns to the bar, refills his glass, and crosses to the phone again.*

*Once more HE dials the Brighton number. Once more HE is baulked.*

*HE jiggles the hook angrily, checks he has the dialling tone, then dials the Exchange.*)

PETER. Operator—I'm having trouble getting through to Brighton. I know the lines are busy in the mornings—

but I've tried three times now, all I get's the unobtainable. Would you please? 68227. This is 071-577-2609. Quick as you can. (*HE waits with impatience, drumming his fingers on the desk. HE takes a pull at his drink and checks the time. His attention is jerked back.*) Yes? Fault on the line—there would be. Could you keep the call in hand? (*Angrily.*) I know it'll cost! Thank you.

(*HE hangs up, and then looks at the back of his hands. THEY are shaking. HE knocks back his drink.*
*HE is on his way for yet another when HE stops suddenly, staring at the front door.*
*SOMEONE is trying the handle.*
*PETER puts his glass down and stands, watching.*
*After a moment or so Drummond's characteristic KNOCK is heard.*)

DRUMMOND. (*Outside.*) Anybody in?

PETER. (*Moves to the door, lifts the latch, and admits him.*) I said I wanted to be left alone.

DRUMMOND. (*Enters, loosening his football scarf.*) And you meant it, didn't you, dropping the latch and everything?

PETER. Where's Richard?

DRUMMOND. Mr. Shaw's gone on ahead.

PETER. You said you were going with him.

DRUMMOND. I don't have to. (*Loosens his scarf.*) I thought you should hear they've established the cause of death as acute barbiturate intoxication.

PETER. That's what we expected.

DRUMMOND. Now it's official.

PETER. And now perhaps you'll lay off me for a bit. Or is that too much to ask?

DRUMMOND. Just about ties everything up, doesn't it?

PETER. Not too sure, are you? What's the problem?

DRUMMOND. You are, Mr. Conway. Well, your reactions, in a manner of speaking.

PETER. Tell me.

DRUMMOND. Seems to me, you've been too calm and self-controlled, right from the start. There's bound to be a backlash, sooner or later. (*Encouragingly*.) Take a break! Get that big car out and go for a long drive—that often helps.

PETER. I only wish I could. Truth is, I was breathalysed a couple of months ago. Bad luck, that's all; I don't make a habit of drinking and driving.

DRUMMOND. Very wise. (*Almost casually.*) The girl friend must have done all the chauffeuring then when you were out last night?

PETER. Yes. She's a very good driver.

DRUMMOND. Americans often are. Takes a great pride in that Volvo of hers, I'll grant her that.

PETER. How do you know?

DRUMMOND. It's been checked over in Brighton this morning, top to bottom. Showroom condition.

PETER. It usually is.

DRUMMOND. Spotless! No sand, no mud, no nothing. Yet you said you were tearing round in it last night ... when it was raining cats and dogs in Sussex.

PETER. We called at a car-wash; between showers.

DRUMMOND. (*Takes out his notebook.*) They'd remember you, of course—like all those other traders along the coast?

PETER. I doubt it. (*Shrugs.*) Automatic car-wash.

DRUMMOND. Don't come scot-free, do they? (*Opens book.*) You must have bought a token?

PETER. Lori had a spare one in the glove-box.

DRUMMOND. (*Not immediately.*) That sounds as though she was prepared for all emergencies. (*HE puts the notebook away again.*)

PETER. Will that be everything?

DRUMMOND. Everything except—fingerprints ...

PETER. (*Coolly.*) I beg your pardon?

DRUMMOND. The bane of my life, they are—always have been. (*Amiably.*) They've gone over Lori's car with a small-tooth comb and there are no prints anywhere. Not even on the steering-wheel.

PETER. (*Silent for a moment before he can come up with an answer.*) Women drivers usually wear gloves, or hadn't you noticed?

DRUMMOND. D'you know, I never thought of that!

PETER. (*Able to relax now.*) I'm going to have another brandy. Care to join me this time?

DRUMMOND. Thank you—er, if it's not imposing. Seeing everything's all done and dusted, why don't we celebrate? (*HE sits down, making himself completely at home.*)

PETER. No further questions?

DRUMMOND. Only one: got any light ale?

PETER. (*Moves behind the bar.*) Should be some here somewhere—

DRUMMOND. Second shelf down, as I recall.

*(PETER throws him a glance, but DRUMMOND's manner is ingenuous.)*

PETER. I thought policemen weren't supposed to drink on duty?

DRUMMOND. That's a popular fallacy. Ask anybody in CID.

PETER. *(Comes back, bringing him a bottle of beer and a glass tankard.)* It tastes better out of one of these.

DRUMMOND. *(Checks label.)* And it's my favourite brand.

PETER. Cheers.

*(HE turns back to the bar and is glad to replenish his own drink, as DRUMMOND pours ale for himself.)*

DRUMMOND. Now why didn't I think of that before?

PETER. What?

DRUMMOND. Detectives! You used to be the pick of the bunch. Why don't I put all the facts in front of you and ask you for a second opinion?

PETER. Amateur versus professional?

DRUMMOND. *(Grins.)* Yes, in a way.

*(PETER pulls a chair round to face the policeman.*
*HE has had a long hard morning, and is suffering from the effects of lack of sleep and too much drink on an empty stomach; however, HE must steel himself to meet this latest challenge and defeat it.*
*HE sits, squarely.)*

PETER. Ready when you are. Question One?

*(Not in any hurry, DRUMMOND takes a sip of his beer first.)*

DRUMMOND. No suicide note. That's worried me from the beginning. I never met a woman yet who didn't want the last word.

PETER. You found the girl's picture in the bedroom, along with Stella's wedding ring. That speaks for itself surely?

DRUMMOND. Not loud enough. Even an amateur sleuth would call that inference, not proof.

PETER. I'd say that's for the coroner to decide.

*(Slight pause.)*

DRUMMOND. Cheers.

*(THEY drink.)*

PETER. Question Two?

DRUMMOND. On all the evidence, Mrs. Conway was a devoted wife—

PETER. Some time ago, not any longer.

DRUMMOND. Then why did she traipse round London half the night looking for a husband she didn't love?

PETER. She gave up after only a few hours, and came back here with my agent.

DRUMMOND. True. And he wouldn't call in for a drink. I wonder why?

PETER. Ask him—you know where he is. Maybe he was too tired. Maybe he sensed he wasn't wanted. After all, Stella had other plans. Important plans.

DRUMMOND. In that case, why wait till three o'clock in the morning to carry 'em out?

PETER. We don't know for certain what time the pills were taken.

DRUMMOND. We've a pretty good idea. Repposal's very quick-acting, and Forensic estimate the time of death as between two and four. I'd go along with that, in view of certain new evidence from that agent of yours.

PETER. (*Shoots him a look.*) You promised me *all* the facts.

DRUMMOND. Mr. Shaw rang your wife at three a.m.—as near as dammit. She answered the phone herself, and her manner was perfectly normal. Yet according to the police surgeons she was dead within the hour. (*Slight pause.*) What's more, if she planned that—as you suggest—why did she encourage him to ring her back this morning?

PETER. (*Slowly.*) I wasn't aware that she did.

DRUMMOND. It'll be in that sworn statement he's making now.

PETER. (*Gets up and starts to move around, getting rattled.*) Obviously, if she'd given him the slightest hint of what was in her mind, he'd have stopped her; that's only common sense.

DRUMMOND. Maybe. Your wife died of phenobarbitone in whisky, a massive concentration. We know about the pills—I saw the empty bottle, by the bed—but where the devil did that whisky come from?

PETER. They'd been touring all the nightspots, don't forget.

DRUMMOND. Not good enough. Mr. Shaw tells me they were on soft drinks only.

PETER. So when she got back, she made up for it! You've seen the decanter—and her glass. Your chaps told me they were smothered in fingerprints.

DRUMMOND. Hers … and yours.

PETER. (*Ready for this.*) I take care of all the glassware at the bar, rinsing, polishing and so forth. My dabs must be everywhere.

DRUMMOND. (*Gently.*) We don't call 'em "dabs" any more, Mr. Conway: that went out with Dixon of Dock Green. Anyway, point taken. I also grant you the decanter was completely empty.

PETER. There's your answer!

DRUMMOND. It would be, if she hadn't told Mr. Shaw you'd polished off the Scotch before you left. And that's why he wouldn't come in for a nightcap.

PETER. She must have been putting him off—

DRUMMOND. (*Levelly.*) There's no trace of whisky anywhere in this house. No empty bottles in the kitchen. Nothing in the garbage. We've looked.

PETER. (*Remains still, staring at him.*) And that's everything that concerns us?

DRUMMOND. For the moment. (*HE lifts his beer, in a toast.*) The best of British luck. (*HE settles back in his chair, very comfortably.*)

PETER. Are you suggesting someone came in here during the night and deliberately *killed* my wife?

DRUMMOND. I'm suggesting—it's a possibility.

PETER. Despite all the evidence to the contrary?

DRUMMOND. Despite all *indications*.

PETER. Name him.

DRUMMOND. Not yet. Not till we've heard what Inspector Savage makes of it.

*(Pause.)*

PETER. Perhaps you'd explain to me first, how anyone could force sleeping-tablets down a woman's throat against her will?

DRUMMOND. They didn't need to. Repposal happens to be soluble in alcohol. All she had to have was a couple of drinks.

PETER. And how did he get hold of the pills? They're on prescription, as you probably know.

DRUMMOND. Appropriated ... one by one ... over a period. He didn't need all that many.

PETER. You realise only one person could have done such a thing?

DRUMMOND. The thought had occurred to me, yes.

PETER. I ought to warn you, sergeant: if you go on with this and you turn out to be wrong, I could have you kicked out of the Force.

DRUMMOND. No great loss, not on either side.

PETER. All right—let's see how much you've got, before we start calling the shots.

DRUMMOND. Preferring charges, d'you mean?

PETER. First—most of this cockeyed theory is based on what my agent told you, agreed?

DRUMMOND. Mr. Shaw's been most helpful.

PETER. Of course he has. Who was the last person to see Stella alive?

DRUMMOND. He was.

PETER. Who said they only drank Coca-Cola while they were out?

DRUMMOND. "Soft drinks," was the way he put it. We can easily check.

PETER. Who recommended Repposal to her in the first place?

DRUMMOND. Same feller.

PETER. And he can get as many as he wants; all legal and aboveboard, on prescription.

DRUMMOND. Absolutely.

PETER. Who left my wife alone, and rang up hours later? Mr. Shaw did. What if he followed that up by coming round here, bringing his own Scotch, knowing Stella would be by herself? She'd have let him in—any hour—because she trusted him.

DRUMMOND. (*Interested.*) Go on—inspector.

PETER. You've got means and opportunity; all you need is motive. *Jealousy.* He's been after my wife for years—ask him!—but he couldn't have her. And he'd never have got her, not while I stood in the way. (*His look is one of triumph.*)

DRUMMOND. But if you loved anyone as much as that, how could you think of killing them?

(*A beat.*)

PETER. Sometimes what we can't have, we destroy. It's a well-known characteristic of human nature. That's my case. (*HE sits again.*)

DRUMMOND. Thank you. I thoroughly enjoyed that. (*HE leaves his seat, to take his empty tankard back to the bar.*)

PETER. Don't tell me you're finally satisfied?

DRUMMOND. You'd be willing, of course, to testify to your case in a court of law?

PETER. Don't be ridiculous.

DRUMMOND. Not even to save your own skin? (*Turns.*) Because that's what it might amount to.

PETER. He's a pal of mine! Besides, we're only playing detective-games, aren't we? *(Laughs.)* Richard wouldn't hurt a fly.

DRUMMOND. I'm glad to hear it.

PETER. (*Rises.*) And neither would I. All I'm saying is, my theory's just as good as yours; and probably better. Because Richard has no alibi—whereas I was miles away from here last night, and I can prove it.

*(The PHONE rings. DRUMMOND, who is nearer the desk, lifts the receiver.)*

PETER. Hold it.

*(DRUMMOND covers the mouthpiece.)*

PETER. I booked a call to Brighton through the operator. There was a fault on the line, earlier on. Mind if I talk to my material witness, in person?

DRUMMOND. (*Looks down at the phone, and then holds it out.*) Be my guest.

PETER. (*Takes over the receiver.*) Lori? (*HE listens for a moment. His expression changes.*) Wrong again. It's the police station, for you.

DRUMMOND. (*Retrieves the phone.*) Bill Drummond. (*Listens.*) You're sure? That just about wraps it up then. (*HE hangs up and looks at PETER non-committally, doing up his scarf.*)

PETER. Going, sergeant? At long last?

DRUMMOND. That's right, sir; we'll be in touch.

PETER. And you will remember, won't you, I was with Lori *all through the night*?

DRUMMOND. If you insist.

PETER. I don't; but she will.

DRUMMOND. She would if she could. Unfortunately, the girl's in no position to testify.

PETER. You just said she was being questioned—

DRUMMOND. No. I said she'd been picked up; I never said she was talking.

PETER. What does that mean?

DRUMMOND. When the Brighton police called at Winchester Terrace this morning, they found Lorraine Helga Nilsson in a state of coma. She'd been violently attacked and was suffering from multiple head-injuries. She was removed to Brighton General Hospital, where she died ten minutes ago—without regaining consciousness.

(*PETER takes a seat again, hardly able to believe his own senses.*)

DRUMMOND. That's why there's been a fault on the line. You see, whoever killed her used her own telephone—to smash her skull.

PETER. (*The moment of truth.*) Stella.

DRUMMOND. They're checking Mrs. Conway's fingerprints now.

PETER. She went out again after Richard had gone. When she got back in the middle of the night, she told me she'd been for a long drive and everything was over—finished.

DRUMMOND. (*Leans forward in his chair.*) Now how could she possibly have done that—*if you hadn't been here at three o'clock, waiting for her?*

(*Pause.*)

PETER. I was. I admit it. She came home to take her own life, to pay for what she'd done. I didn't realise the truth until it was too late. (*HE drags himself to his feet, his voice devoid of emotion.*) Shall we go?

DRUMMOND. Not yet. I can't make an arrest till all the confirmations are in.

PETER. Going by the book, eh? Savage believed in that.

DRUMMOND. Meanwhile, please don't leave the house.

PETER. I wouldn't get very far, would I? Seeing I'll be under strict surveillance.

DRUMMOND. Playing the murder game, aren't we, sir? What do you expect? (*HE leaves.*)

(*PETER crosses to the bar and swigs more brandy. This time HE drinks straight from the bottle, liquor dribbling unheeded down his chin.*

*A POLICEMAN in uniform crosses the window, on his way to take up a station outside the front door.*
*PETER sees him.*
*HE wipes his mouth roughly on his sleeve and stands alone, swaying on his feet, now there is no longer anyone else to see or care. Underlying tension and excess of alcohol have induced in him a mental state that is dangerous; not only to others, but also—though HE is unaware of this—to himself.)*

PETER. (*Viciously.*) Bastard.

*(HE drains the bottle, and flings the now useless object behind the bar, where it shatters in pieces.*
*HE goes to the display shelves at the rear, to take something down from there. We cannot be sure of what this is until he has crossed the room, to gaze up at the portrait of himself as "Savage" on the wall.)*

PETER. Little man … big finish.

*(His hand comes into view and we realise HE is holding the old razor he has treasured for years. The blade is open.*
*With one deft movement HE slashes the razor across his throat.*
*For an instant HE twists in agony, but it is long enough for us to see the spurt of blood. Then HE crashes headlong towards us.*
*The once-famous Inspector Savage has made his final exit.*
*SWELL THEME MUSIC suddenly to full.)*

**SLOW CURTAIN**

## COSTUME  PLOT

### PETER
Act I, Sc.l.
White shirt under light sweater.
Dark slacks. Black moccasins.
NO CHANGE THROUGHOUT

### STELLA
Act I, Sc.l.
Pinafore, over colourful shirt.
Blue jeans.
Mules.

CHANGE TO:
Elegant, fashionable dress.
Town coat with matching accessories.

Act I, Sc.2.
Dark business suit, smart but not expensive.

Act II, Sc.l.
White mackintosh over street-outfit.
No head-covering.

CHANGE TO:
Plain housecoat.
Slippers.

### DRUMMOND
Act I, Sc.l.
Car coat, over cardigan.

Grey slacks.
Chelsea Football Club scarf.

Act II, Sc.2.
Serviceable grey suit, quiet tie.
Raglan raincoat.

**LORI**
Act I,Sc.l.
Sexy costume, suitable for hostess working at cheap night-club.

CHANGE TO:
Simple but smart afternoon dress.

Act II, Sc.2.
Tight sweater and modish slacks.
Carry wind-cheater and tote bag.

**RICHARD**
Act II, Sc.2.
Light d.b. suit, well-tailored.

**DRESSER**
Act I, Sc.l.
Green warehouse-coat, with "BBC" embroidered in red on top pocket.
Navy-blue slacks.
Brown suede shoes.

## PROPERTY PLOT
(Essentials)

### ACT I, Scene 1
Set Onstage
Desk:

>Photographs of Peter and Stella.
>Penholder, with pens and pencils.
>Cigarette-box, stocked.
>Table lighter.
>Medical cards, in drawer.

Bar:

>Brandy (practical).
>White wine (practical).
>Whisky decanter, quarter full (practical).
>Bottle of light ale (shelf behind).
>Ice bucket.
>Soda syphon.
>Hand-towels.

Hi-Fi

>Audio-tape.

Disp. Shelves

>Cut-throat razor in ornamental case.

Cloaks Cupboard

>Sheepskin coat (Peter).
>Driving gloves in coat pocket.

Set Offstage.
Folding stool (Lori).
Telescript (Lori).
Cardboard cup of tea (Lori).
Hefty paperback book (Lori).
Coat (Lori).

Used glass (Lori).
Handbag (Lori).
  In it—Postcard photo. Papermate pen.
Grey trench-coat (Dresser).
Tweed hat (Dresser).
Scotch-on-the-rocks (Dresser).
Black document-case (Richard).
Check:
Windows shut.
Curtains shut.
Doors shut.

**ACT I, Scene 2**
Strike: No strike.
Set: No set.

Check:
Clean ashtrays.
Windows shut.
Curtains shut.
Doors shut.

**ACT II, Scene 1**
Strike: No strike.

Set.
  Bar: Whisky decanter, now half-full.
  Armchair: Turn to face upstage.
Check:
Windows shut.
Curtains shut.
Doors shut.

**ACT II, Scene 2**
Strike:
> Desk  Empty phial.
> Decanter.
> Used whisky glass.
> Postcard photo (Lori).

Reset:
Armchair to normal.

Set:
Armchair: Drummond's scarf.

Check:
Windows shut.
Curtains open.
Doors shut.

## PERSONAL PROPS

(Essentials)

### PETER
Cigarettes and lighter, identical with those used by Drummond.
Wrist-watch.

### STELLA
Wedding ring.
Empty phial.
Handbag.

**DRUMMOND**
Cigarettes and lighter, identical with those used by Peter.
Warrant card.
Notebook.
Retractable biro pen.
Postcard photo of Lori, signed.
Wedding ring, identical with Stella's.
Rimless spectacles in leather case.
Police receipt-form.

**LORI**
Tote bag.
In it:
       Set of car keys.
       Pack of American cigarettes.
       Book matches.

# Other Publications For Your Interest

**RAVENSCROFT. (Little Theatre.) Mystery.** Don Nigro. 1m., 5f. Simple unit set. This unusual play is several cuts above the genre it explores, a Gothic thriller for groups that don't usually do such things, a thinking person's mystery, a dark comedy that is at times immensely funny and at others quite frightening. On a snowy night, Inspector Ruffing is called to a remote English country house to investigate the headlong plunge of a young manservant, Patrick Roarke, down the main staircase, and finds himself getting increasingly involved in the lives of five alluring and dangerous women— Marcy, the beautiful Viennese governess with a past, Mrs. Ravenscroft, the flirtatious and chattery lady of the manor, Gillian, her charming but possibly demented daughter, Mrs. French, the formidable and passionate cook, and Dolly, a frantic and terrified little maid—who lead him through an increasingly bewildering labyrinth of contradictory versions of what happened to Patrick and to the dead Mr. Ravenscroft before him. There are ghosts at the top of the staircase, skeletons in the closet, and much more than the Inspector had bargained for as his quest to solve one mystery leads him deeper and deeper into others and to an investigation of his own tortured soul and the nature of truth itself. You will not guess the ending, but you will be teased, seduced, bewildered, amused, frightened and led along with the Inspector to a dark encounter with truth, or something even stranger. A funny, first rate psychological mystery, and more.

**(#19987)**

**DARK SONNETS OF THE LADY, THE. (Advanced Groups.) Drama.** Don Nigro. 4m., 4f. Unit set. First produced professionally at the McCarter Theatre in Princeton and a finalist for the National Play Award, this stunningly theatrical and very funny drama takes place in Vienna in the fall of the year 1900, when Dora, a beautiful and brilliant young girl, walks into the office of Sigmund Freud, then an obscure doctor in his forties, to begin the most famous and controversial encounter in the history of psychoanalysis. Dora is funny, suspicious, sarcastic and elusive, and Freud become fascinated and obsessed by her and by the intricate labyrinth of her illness. He moves like a detective through the mystery of her life, and we meet in the course of his journey through her mind: her lecherous father, her obsessively house-cleaning mother, her irritating brother, her sinister admirer Herr Klippstein and his sensual and seductive wife, and their pretty and lost little governess. Nightmares, fantasies, hallucinations and memories all come alive onstage in a wild kaleidoscopic tapestry as Freud moves closer and closer to the truth about Dora's murky past, and the play becomes a kind of war between the two of them about what the truth is, about the uneasy truce between men and women, and ultimately a tragic love story. Laced throughout with eerie and haunting Strauss waltzes, this is a rich, complex, challenging and delightfully intriguing universe, a series of riddles one inside the other that lead the audience step by step to the center of Dora's troubled soul and her innermost secrets. Is Dora sick, or is the corrupt patriarchal society in which she and Freud are both trapped the real source of a complex group neurosis that binds all the characters together in a dark web of desperate erotic relationships, a kind of beautiful, insane and terrible dance of life, desire and death? **(#5952)**

# New Thrillers from
# Samuel French, Inc.

**ACCOMPLICE. (Little Theatre). Thriller.** Rupert Holmes. 2m., 2f., plus one surprise guest star. Int. This truly unique new thriller by the author *The Mystery of Edwin Drood* broke all box office records at the Pasadena Playhouse, and went on to thrill audiences on Broadway. Sorry, but the only way we can describe the amazing plot for you is to "give it away." *Accomplice* starts out as a straightforward English thriller, set in a country house, in which a sex-starved wife plans, with the help of her lover, to murder her stuffy husband. All is, of course, not as it first seems. Oh, yes!— the "husband" is murdered onstage; but, later, he re-enters! Why? Because what we have actually been watching is a dress rehearsal. The play takes a new twist when we learn that this is an out-of-town tryout. The "husband" we have just seen "murdered" is actually the playwright and director of the play-within-the-play, and *he* has plotted to murder his *wife,* the actress playing the lead in his play, so that he can proceed unimpeded with his affair with her leading man. Got that so far? Well—you ain't seen *nothing* yet! A surprise character comes out of the audience (no—we won't tell you who it is), revealing that, in actuality, something entirely different is going on. A cast member is being set up—brilliantly and effectively, it turns out; and the cast has its final revenge against a fellow thespian whose cruelty resulted in the suicide of a friend. "The show is a delight. It is humorous, odd, scary, wildly dramatic, adult, adolescent— in short, impossible to dislike."—Pasadena Star-News. "Miss it at your peril."—L.A. Herald Examiner. "Wonderfully entertaining . . . a breathless ride through an ever-shifting series of planes."—Cleveland Plain Dealer. "A total delight."—Bergen News. "Part murder mystery, part sex farce and completely entertaining . . . suspenseful, charming and funny."—USA Today. Slightly restricted.                    (#3144)

**MAKING A KILLING. (Little Theatre.) Thriller.** John Nassivera. 2m., 2f. Comb. Int. A Broadway playwright, his conniving producer and his actress wife hatch a plot to guarantee their new play will be a success; they fake the suicide of the playwright on opening night! They then high-tail it up to Vermont where the playwright hopes to disappear, as he hates the public spotlight anyway. However, after a few weeks the playwright decides he no longer wants to participate in the scheme. Maybe his wife and his producer (who are having an affair) will have to kill him for real! Also on the scene is the playwright's feisty agent, who uncovers the plot and then helps her client deal with his most difficult artistic challenge: foiling his producer and wife! "A magnificent mystery thriller ... wonderful entertainment."—Bennington Banner. "Absorbing theatre."—Schenectady Gazette.                    (#15200)